W. H. Parkins

How I Escaped

a Novel

W. H. Parkins

How I Escaped
a Novel

ISBN/EAN: 9783337047153

Printed in Europe, USA, Canada, Australia, Japan

Cover: Foto ©Andreas Hilbeck / pixelio.de

More available books at **www.hansebooks.com**

HOW I ESCAPED

A Novel

BY

W. H. PARKINS

EDITED BY

ARCHIBALD CLAVERING GUNTER

AUTHOR OF

"MR. BARNES OF NEW YORK"

"MR. POTTER OF TEXAS," ETC

NEW YORK

THE HOME PUBLISHING COMPANY

7 EAST FOURTEENTH STREET

1889.

Press of J. J. Little & Co.
Astor Place, New York.

CONTENTS.

BOOK IV.

HOW I CAME BACK AND FOUGHT FOR HER.

HOW I ESCAPED.

BOOK I.

How I Stayed for Her.

CHAPTER I.

"GOT YOUR CARPET-BAG PACKED?"

"LAURA—Miss Peyton, may I have a dance?"

"Certainly!"

"The next waltz?"

"No—the next *dance*, whatever it is! Please take the very next, and come with me now."

As she said this, Laura Peyton slipped her arm into mine, and leading me through one of the French windows of the old southern house onto the wide balcony, whispered, her blue eyes blazing with excitement in the moonlight, though her cheeks were pale and her lips trembled: "Lawrence, it has come!"

"Do you really mean it?"

"Yes, South Carolina has seceded!"

Her words brought almost despair to my heart, for Laura Peyton was a southern girl and I a northern man; and though but the day before we had plighted our troths and given our loves, I trembled as I thought of what the political passions of the time might bring to our lives.

Seeing my expression, Laura suddenly placed her hand in mine, and whispered: "This shall never alter my promise to you, Lawrence!"

Some girls would have blushed or fluttered with a perhaps unconscious coquetry as they said the words, for this was the second time in her life that my *fiancée* had called me by my Christian name ; but Laura Peyton's voice was firm and resolute, and brought back to me a firmness that I must confess for a moment had left me, for I knew the passion that was dominant in the South in 1860, and the manner in which northern men were regarded by a large number of the population south of Mason and Dixon's line.

Some of this spirit was observable as we reëntered the house, where a few of Laura's young friends were enjoying an informal carpet-dance in the large old-fashioned parlor that December evening. Judge Peyton's residence was about five miles away from the little capital of South Carolina, and the sudden cessation of the music and excited exclamations of the guests told us that the news had become generally known to the company.

Belle, Laura's younger sister, who had been playing one of those old, long-since-forgotten Jullien polkas, after a moment's pause suddenly attacked the piano again with all the enthusiasm of sixteen, and sang the local secession air that was soon afterward superseded by the *Bonnie Blue Flag* with her whole soul. The effect was electrical, and in a moment every voice in the room except my own rang out with the southern air.

My failure to respond to this outburst of secession sentiment was noted by a young lawyer, who had been my friend and chum until a rivalry for Laura's affections and hand had somewhat cooled our good-fellowship. Harry Walton stepped up to me, and rather insinuatingly remarked : " Mr. Bryant does not sing this evening. Has he lost his voice ? "

" No," I replied ; " but I don't know that tune."

" It's one that you'll have to sing before long, and if necessary I'll try and teach it to you," sneered young Walton.

" Oh, I'll instruct Law—Mr. Bryant myself," interrupted Laura, anxious to change a conversation that was becoming of a nature that sometimes in those days led to very serious results.

This stumble over my Christian name probably enraged my rival much more than my refusal to join in the secession melody.

An expression of trouble passed over his face, as he

caught a veiled glance the girl at my side cast upon me as she interposed between us. He bit his lip, and remarked coldly, with a forced composure: "Then I leave Mr. Bryant to your instructions, Miss Laura; but in case you do not succeed—there are other and stronger teachers——"

"None that you could bring to bear upon me, Mr. Walton," I remarked. "If Miss Peyton does not succeed, *you* had better not attempt the task."

My rival was about to reply in a tone that might have led to unpleasant results, when the conversation was interrupted by the entrance of Judge Peyton, the father of my sweetheart, and the company of young people running to him to get his ideas upon the political situation.

"Father, you've heard the news! We're no longer in the United States. We've cut loose from Uncle Sam. Seceded at last!" cried his son, young Arthur Peyton, with the enthusiasm of twenty.

"Yes; I've expected this for months," returned the judge solemnly, "and feared it!"

"Feared it?" echoed two or three of the guests.

"Feared it," cried his son; "feared the Yankees? Why Alabama, Mississippi, Louisiana, Georgia—every southern State is with us. We've all the trump cards in this game!"

"Humph!" returned the judge. "But we haven't played them. We'll all do our duty by our State, Arthur; but I'm afraid there'll be more tears than laughter about this business before it is ended."

With those words and a slight sigh, Judge Peyton turned to his study, and after a few moments the company gradually left for their homes.

"I shall. see your father in a day or two, Laura," I whispered as I bid her good-by. "This political complication compels me to have no misunderstanding in my relations to you."

"You—you know I love you—will love you, no matter what happens," returned my *fiancée*.

Then mounting my horse for my short ride to Columbia, I saw Laura watching me as I passed down the moonlit avenue, the girl making a very pretty picture backgrounded by her southern home.

Laura Peyton though in some respects a typical

southern girl, had little of that languor supposed to be peculiar to tropical loveliness, was no brunette with black lustrous eyes and voluptuous, lazy beauty, but brilliant and blue-eyed, vigorous and direct in movement and mind, and of a beauty that made her a female load-stone to the local beaux. Perhaps from very force of contrast to the languid manners of most of the South Carolina girls about her, she was one of the most popular young ladies in the section of the State near Columbia.

It was a short five miles to the capital. I let my horse take his own gait, while I meditated upon the problem before me—that was to win and marry a southern girl from a southern family—from a seceded State, I—a northern man—a Union man, one who might have to meet her relatives even in battle—and this in December of the year 1860, with the passions of that gigantic political volcano seething and struggling and fighting to break out of the crater that had been opened that very day by the secession of South Carolina. Pondering upon this problem I trotted into the main street of Columbia, which was full of excited people discussing the situation, and as I did so, started and listened.

The city bell upon the old market was ringing out joyous peal upon peal that meant its own and that town's destruction by sword and flame after four years of most miserable horror and bloody war to the American people.

The excitement had spread to the negro population. Young Caucus, my body servant, came to me, his eyes rolling and his red hair more frizzled than usual with excitement, for he was a mulatto with that unusual hair in people of his race, that we call brick-red. This gave him a curious made-up appearance, and added a comedy look to the boy even when he was in a rage.

As young Caucus, whose services I had hired from his master, Judge Peyton, took charge of my horse, he seemed choking with some extraordinary idea, which had just come into his black brain, and gasped out to me: "'Skuse me, Massa Bryant, but what you s'pose Massa Abram Lincoln do now dat South Carlina commit 'cession—reckon Massa Lincoln hab to commit sucide."

This extraordinary idea of the President elect's political duties made but little impression upon me at the moment. I was too much perplexed at my own position, though I have often laughed at it since.

I declined to discuss the matter with young Caucus, and passed into my house, where I spent several wakeful hours that night pondering over love, politics, and patriotism.

I had been about five years in the South, having been called there in my profession of civil engineer to assist in laying out the work and building some of the new railroads being constructed in South Carolina and Georgia. I liked the country and its people, and did not wish to leave it—in fact, would not leave it unless I took Laura Peyton to the North with me, as a hostage from the southern people. Yet as I faced the outlook, and thought of having that very day been almost cut in the street by people I had considered as intimates, because they doubted my loyalty to the cause of secession, and remembered the speeches made since Lincoln's election, I could not doubt that my next few months would be unpleasant ones in the Palmetto State, and that my course of true love would run over one of the rockiest beds that was ever invented for that tumultuous and uncertain stream.

Pondering on this problem, I fell asleep, to be aroused next morning by the voice of Tom Baxter, who cried to me in a cheery way, " Got your carpet-bag packed ? "

" No !—what do you mean ? "

" Well, you'll have to pack it soon. I mean you and I'll have to go North."

Tom was my associate engineer, and, occupying the same house with me, ejaculated his words from the next bedroom, where he was apparently making his morning ablutions.

" You've just arrived from Augusta ? " asked I.

" One hour ago. And they're getting ready to do the same job in Georgia that they did in South Carolina yesterday. Tell you more about it at breakfast," remarked the sententious Tom.

Baxter had come from Illinois. Like myself, he saw the storm ahead, though from a different point of view, as he had been for the last few weeks, on the business of the railroad, in Georgia. He was a hard-thinking fellow, and reasoned upon all subjects, professional and otherwise, with the directness of a mathematician and in a very straight line.

I was anxious to get his full views upon our situation, and followed him quickly to our breakfast-room.

As I entered, Mr. Baxter was laughing at some remarks of young Caucus, who was waiting at the table.

" How you tink, Massa Baxter, de North stan up agin dose ? " exclaimed the negro, giving an excited wave of his napkin through the open window toward three companies of South Carolina militia that were marching by with true militia irregularity. " Dose sogers go up to settle de Black 'Publicans and dey settle dem abolitionists d——d soon ! "

" Give me some eggs ! " said Baxter, choking a laugh.

" Some eggs and coffee for me, also, Caucus, and then get out," added I ; " I wish to talk to Mr. Baxter."

" Yes sah ! of course sah ! " muttered the young negro, executing our orders, and then retiring from the room with martial step and a grin of joy, for the military band outside had suddenly struck up, and Caucus was anxious to follow the music, which he did shortly afterward, together with half the young negroes of Columbia.

" Now," remarked Baxter, as soon as the sound of Caucus' departing footsteps had died away, " you and I, Lawrence, will have to take a trip north very shortly. I suppose you are aware of that ? South Carolina seceded yesterday. To-morrow it will be Georgia and all the cotton States. And you and I know on which side of the line we ought to be when it comes to fighting."

" I shall remain here, at least for the present," I remarked.

" So shall I, but I shall sell everything I have and be prepared to leave. Take my advice, and do the same."

" Still, I'm comfortable here ; have succeeded in my profession ; am popular with the people about me."

" Popular ?—How long will you be popular if you don't take their side in the coming struggle ? Popular ?— Doesn't every day show you your popularity is waning ? Popular ?——"

Here he stopped short, for Caucus came into the room bringing a pretty little envelope addressed to me in a feminine hand.

As I tore open the envelope and devoured its contents, Mr. Baxter continued :

" Popular—yes, I see, very popular with some one about here. That's why you're so anxious to stay. Well, if I guess right as to who the lady is, I'd risk a good deal to gain that girl, for she's worth winning. I wish you luck; but all the same, if you remain in this State, you'll have to fight on one side of the line and I on the other, for I tell you that this movement means *war !* "

" WAR ? "

" Certainly ! Isn't that "—here Mr. Baxter got up from his chair, walked round to mine, and whispered in my ear —" armed rebellion to our Government—levying of war upon it right there before our very eyes ? " and he pointed through the window, toward where a portion of the South Carolina militia were marching down the main street of Columbia to take the cars for Charleston, to participate a short time afterward in the bombardment of Sumter.

" It's war! " he continued—" miserable, horrible, bloody civil war ! You've got to take your choice—our side or the other ; and if you remain here, it must be the other."

" All the same," I replied, " I shall stay here until——"

" Until you win her ? I wish you luck, my boy ; but she a southern girl and you a northern man—God help you ! " And with this Mr. Baxter turned away, walked out of the room and went to his work at the railroad offices.

I remained with a very glum face, which became more gloomy as I re-read the letter my *fiancée* had just written to me. It was as follows :

" ' THE OAKS,'   }
COLUMBIA, *December* 21, 1860. ∫

" DARLING : Please come and see papa this very afternoon at the latest. Circumstances that I cannot explain by letter make me ask you as you love me not to delay your interview with my father. To-morrow may be too late. Don't fail.

" YOUR LAURA."

What new complication did this note herald ? Puzzle my brain as I might, I could not guess. Of only one thing was I sure—that was my sweetheart loved me. So despite the clouds that seemed to hang over me, I was, in the elasticity of youth, comparatively happy even on that morning.

But curiosity, added to love, made me hurry what

little railroad business I had on my hands, and early in the afternoon I rode out through the main street of Columbia, which was filled with people eagerly discussing the situation, for nearly all business was thrown aside for politics at that time, and after passing by the State lunatic asylum and the beautiful plantations of the Hamptons, Prestons and Singletons, soon found myself at the Avenue of Oaks that led to Judge Peyton's country seat, called after the beautiful trees that embellished it.

Before I reached the house, however, I was met by Miss Belle, who came running down the avenue to meet me, a leghorn hat with ribbons floating from it, after the fashion of the time, in one hand, the other held out to me. In the frank impulsiveness of her nature, she cried, with the very sweet southern accent this young lady possessed, " Laura has just told me all."

" All ! " I muttered, astonished at the suddenness of her outburst.

" Certainly—all about you're wanting to marry her ! " You see she had to—a girl must confide in some one— no one could keep such a secret—and mother being dead, I took mamma's place—and I'm so glad you're going to join us—be one of us—I always said that Mr. Bryant was too good a man to be one of those awful Black Republicans—'deed I did ! "

This view of my political ideas being changed by my suit for her sister's hand rather amused me. I remarked :

" I have never been a Black Republican—that is, not the kind of a Black Republican you mean."

" There's only one kind of Black Republican ! " returned Miss Belle, sententiously.

" What kind is that ? "

" A bad abolitionist Black Republican. Oh, how I hate 'em. They would destroy all our social happiness. They would separate us from the servants who love us. Fancy tearing old Mauma Chloe from me whom she loves. I told the poor old creature what the horrid northern wretches wanted to do to her, and she cried all last night. But you're reformed—I know you are—and—you would like to see Laura, I suppose—she rather expects you "— this last with a roguish glance. " She's over there in the garden ! Here, Cæsar ! come and take Mr. Bryant's horse ! "

I dismounted, and a black servant leading my nag to the stables, Miss Belle pointed to a white hat seen through the foliage, and cried, " There she is ! Good-by till—afterward, Mr. Reformed Black Republican ! "

I hardly heard the last of her speech, as I was rapidly making my way toward my sweetheart, who apparently did not notice my coming. As seated upon a bench in a little grove of oaks, she held a letter in her hand, though both her eyes were expectantly placed upon the road from Columbia. She had in some manner apparently missed me as I rode by, and was still looking for my coming—I thought with a kind of nervous impatience.

A man's vanity is always flattered by the beauty of the woman who loves him ; and in gazing at Laura Peyton I became very vain, for no prettier sight had ever met my eye.

Though nearly Christmas, the weather was still mild and warm in this southern latitude, and the girl looked like a summer picture, as, with her white hat trimmed with a dainty ribbon or two thrown upon the bench beside her, and dressed in some light gossamer garment crinolined and puffed out about her, as was the fashion of those days, she leaned forward, all her soul in her eyes, looking the wrong way—for *me*.

A moment afterward the tableau changed. Her eyes fell upon the letter—a shiver of disgust appeared to run through her. She sprang to her feet impatiently, in her haste permitting a glimpse of a southern foot and ankle that gave me another lover's rapture, and crushed the letter nervously in her hand. Her lips muttered in an excited manner, her eyebrows contracted with a slight frown, and she gave a determined stamp with her little foot.

Then she turned her head, the frown changed to a smile, the shadow on her face became sunshine, her lips murmured, " Lawrence ! "—she was in my arms.

After a moment she disengaged herself from my embrace, and, affecting lightness, whispered : " I knew you would come. My note insured that. Curiosity as well as love is powerful in man as in woman."

" Why were you so anxious for me to see your father this very day ? " I asked, in reply to this.

" This letter ! " she said, glancing at the crumpled paper.

"To-night, or at latest to-morrow, Amos Pierson will ask my father for my hand. This is his notification to me of his intention."

"Amos Pierson !" I gasped—"the millionaire cotton merchant of Savannah ?"

"Certainly," she replied. "He entertained my father and myself last year when we visited Georgia. I think—I fear—he has some business or financial hold upon my father !"

"You surely do not believe Judge Peyton would coerce you—in such a matter as this !"

"Certainly not ! But Amos Pierson, I can see from his letter, expects in the arrogance of his wealth to win me. Disappointment will make him our enemy and at this moment we need so many friends ! Lawrence, I know his character—*beware of Amos Pierson !*"

CHAPTER II.

AMOS PIERSON.

"BEWARE of Amos Pierson—why ?—because he is my rival ? What do I fear, so long as I have your love ? Laura, why don't you ask me to dread all the suitors for this hand—Harry Walton, for instance ?" replied I, seizing the fair member she had held out in warning gesture.

"Because Harry Walton is a gentleman—impulsive, but always chivalric, always brave. Brave men are not so much to be dreaded as cowards. They strike fairly to your face—not behind your back. Amos Pierson is one of the kind you feel, but do not see. He will wound you in the back !"

"Pshaw ! I'd much rather have Amos Pierson for a rival for your hand than Harry Walton—fifty is not so much to be dreaded as twenty-five, and I have heard Mr. Pierson's age stated at about the former figure," laughed I, anxious to relieve the anxiety of my *fiancée*, though by no means happy to hear of an additional enemy to my wooing, surrounded as it was with so many political obstacles.

"Therefore you understand the reason I wish you to see my father this afternoon—so that Mr. Pierson, when he arrives, will discover that my future station in life is already settled. That "—here she began to blush and falter—"that—I am as surely and as truly yours as if I were already wedded to—you!"

The last "you" was a little gasp, for what man could refrain from *sealing* such a declaration from the woman he loved?

"So," I replied, "you wish Mr. Pierson to know he has no hope——"

"At once and forever! You will find my father, Lawrence, in his library. This action of South Carolina has disturbed him very much. Heaven only knows to what it will lead!"

Knowing the house very well, I turned from my sweetheart and found my way to her father, meditating on the consideration of Laura, who, in all our interview, had never mentioned the political troubles that stood in our path almost forcing us asunder; for my sweetheart's sympathies were all with the South in the struggle, as what southern woman's were not, through that four years of famine, desolation, flame and bereavement,—to the end!

I knew, however, her father would mention the political aspect of our courtship, and was prepared for it.

On entering Judge Peyton's library, to my astonishment I found him with the day's papers before him and a suspicious redness about the eyes. He greeted me pleasantly, but rather sadly.

"You have been reading the news?" I ventured to remark, "with a good deal of interest."

"With a good deal of sorrow," he replied. "This ordinance of our State legislature is, I feel, perhaps wrong—certainly hasty; and may bring us more trouble than our politicians reckon. They pass the ordinance, but if it comes to fighting, the people will have to do that, and I have a young boy "—here the judge looked wistfully at the picture of Arthur that hung upon the wall; then continued with a sigh—"and he is anxious to be in the front. I fear for him. Heaven only knows what secession **may** bring to my family!"

Here was my opening. I remarked:

"It was in regard to your family that I called to speak to you.   Miss Laura——"

"Ah!"

"I love her, and I have asked her to marry me.   She has consented.   I have now come to you to ask your approval of my suit."

To this the judge did not answer, so I went on and gave him a short history of my courtship of his daughter, stating that our affection was mutual.

Here the judge stopped me by remarking, suddenly, "You wish to marry my daughter at *this* time?"

"As soon as possible!   You know my professional reputation in the South: that I am as well able to support her as most young men who depend entirely upon their professional exertions."

"Yes, I have no doubt of your ability," replied the old gentleman, "as an engineer; but, though I have every respect for your professional attainments, the peculiar position that you hold in our community makes me hesitate to give my consent to your proposition that a few months ago I should have been pleased to consider."

"Why should the severance by South Carolina of her ties to the Federal Government of the United States compel me to sever the ties of love that bind me to your daughter?" I asked, impetuously.

"Because the ordinance of secession passed yesterday will make my daughter and you citizens of two different nations that bid fair, shortly, to become hostile to one another.   If war should break out between us and the United States, you would be unable to live in this community, and a wife must follow her husband," remarked the judge, slowly and deliberately, as if weighing his words.   "My daughter's sympathies are, I hope, entirely with the people of her State in such a quarrel.   Political differences would destroy eventually any love that there now may be between you.   You are both young, impulsive, and ardent, and you could not so entirely restrain yourselves as to prevent the excitement of the combat raging about you from entering into your home.   Therefore I am opposed to any immediate union between you and my daughter.   Perhaps," continued the judge, with a sigh, "this quarrel of the politicians may yet be settled by the people without bloodshed.   Pray heaven it may be ! If so, come to me again, and if my daughter loves you as you say she does, my answer will be a different one, unless——"

" Unless what ? " I interrupted, hastily.

" Unless "——here he checked himself suddenly and said : " But that is an affair of the future. At present all I can say, Mr. Bryant, is, that I wish you to consider my daughter entirely freed from any promise she has made to you until the present political storm has ended. God knows I wish South Carolina had not seceded ! " he continued, impulsively.

"Ah ! ycu are a Union man," I cried.

" I love the Union, but I love my State better ; and though, like many other men in the South, I have struggled to prevent yesterday's hasty and radical action by my native commonwealth ; still, that action being taken, I am for my State, *right or wrong.* I shall confer with Laura, and perhaps, after an interview with her may write you further my views upon the proposition you have done me the honor to make. You have my highest personal esteem, Mr. Bryant," he said, shaking my hand as I rose with rather a gloomy and unhappy expression on my face.

"Then you have no objection to my visiting your daughter ? " I asked.

"None in the world, *as a friend.* All I wish is that until the political horizon becomes clear, you entirely forget that my daughter has given you reason to hope for her hand. As a man of common sense, this should impress itself upon you. As a man of honor, a father's wishes in regard to his child at such a moment should be binding upon you." With this the judge returned to his reading, apparently anxious to close the interview.

As I walked through the hallway I encountered a young gentleman whom I hoped would some day be my brother-in-law—young Mr. Arthur Peyton, with the enthusiasm of twenty, excitement, youth and hope upon his face, had apparently just arrived from Columbia.

His expression betokened intense joy. He cried out merrily : " Hello, Bryant ! Isn't this glorious ? Wade Hampton is about to raise a legion for the service of South Carolina in case of northern invasion, and has

2

offered me a lieutenancy. There's promotion for you! Quicker than if I had been at West Point."

" If the uniform is handsome, I presume you'll be very fatal to the young ladies about here," remarked I.

" Trust me for that," laughed the boy, and continued : " By the bye, your friend Walton will rank me, as he has been offered a captaincy."

" That is the advantage of twenty-five over twenty in this world."

" But I don't suppose you care much about this, as you are a northern man; though perhaps, pleaded with "—here the rogue winked at me—" by my sister, we may consider you as not the *worst* type of ' Black Republican.' "

These remarks, which brought me once more face to face with the obstacle constantly growing larger and larger between my love and its happy consummation, gave me a very surly and dogged air as I walked into the garden, which was instantly perceived by my *fiancée*.

As she came toward me, she whispered : " Lawrence, bad news ? Papa refuses his consent ? "

" Not so bad as that," I replied. " He only asks us to postpone our engagement until our political troubles are ended."

" Postpone our engagement ? You mean postpone our marriage."

" No—our engagement ! "

" Impossible ! Our engagement was made yesterday. As well ask us to postpone our love."

" Yes, he asks us to forget what we said to each other yesterday. Can you do that ? " I whispered into the dainty shell that she called her ear.

" Forget that you said you loved me ?—Oh, Lawrence ! " and the tears came into her eyes.

" That is what he asks ; but it is as impossible for me as to forget that I live. However, that is what your father wants."

" I can forget no more than you that I love you ! " whispered the dear girl, emphasizing her words with a glance that set me to comforting her in the way most pleasing to engaged young ladies.

After a few moments, her spirits having come back to her, Miss Laura said, airily : " Oh, I don't mind if papa asks us to postpone our marriage, after all ! "

"Indeed!" I said, rather sullenly. "I had supposed you wished to marry me immediately."

"No, Lawrence, not *immediately*," said the young lady, laughing. "*Trousseaux* are works of time, and by the time my *trousseau* is ready, this political squabble between our southern fire-eating politicians and your Puritanical northern philanthropists will undoubtedly be ended. So when my *trousseau* is ready, I shall be ready. As to the engagement being suspended, I will see papa about that at once"—this with a little laugh and playful threatening of the hand toward the judge's library window.

"Immediately?" I cried, in rapture.

"Yes," she said, starting and turning pale. "This matter must be settled within five minutes, for I see the man who will do all he can to prevent our union from being made complete." As she said this she pointed down the avenue, and following the direction of her hand, I saw a gentleman riding up the pretty road that led from Columbia.

"His name?" I gasped.

"Amos Pierson," she faltered, and with that disappeared by one of the French windows leading from the old-fashioned southern portico into her father's library.

I gazed very savagely at this supposed enemy of my happiness as he rode up the avenue, and did not think him handsome.

He was a man about fifty years of age, rather inclined to be florid and stout, with brilliant steel-blue eyes, an honest forehead, but a treacherous mouth. He frequently laughed, and showed exceedingly white, large fangy teeth. He was dressed in the southern style of that day, in black broadcloth somewhat too large for him, dark slouch hat, pronounced diamonds and massive gold jewelry in the form of rings and watch-chain. He was followed by a handsome young quadroon slave, carrying a valise and saddle-bags upon the horse he rode at a short distance behind his master.

"Ain't he horrid?" whispered Miss Belle in my ear, as she came beside me to witness the new arrival. "He is like Sol Smith, the actor, when he plays *Jacques Strop*," for this young lady, though but sixteen, had a passionate love for the theater, and regarded a visit to Charleston, where she could see any of the popular pieces of that day, as one of the joys of her existence.

Mr. Pierson, however, not having heard this remark, flashed at the young lady a grinny smile, saluted her with a wave of his hand, and coming up to her, said, enthusiastically : "You have done the business in South Carolina a little ahead of us Georgians, Miss Belle, but we won't be far behind you. These northern abolitionists who would rob us of our property must be checked at once and forever."

These remarks from a man who had not yet lost his New England twang, and whose every manner and gesture indicated his Yankee origin, seemed to me as astonishing as they were disgusting ; but he was like most northern men who from self-interest or association took the part of the South in our late quarrel ; the further north a man came from, the more bitter, unrelenting, bloodthirsty and cruel he was in his sentiments, expressions, and denunciations of the birth-place that he had disowned and upon which he was willing to make war. This was not so astonishing as it would seem, for nearly all of these men had come down south as slave traders or overseers,—two occupations that did not tend to develop the sympathy and kindliness of the human heart.

Mr. Pierson had begun as overseer some thirty years before I saw him, and from that had graduated to slave dealer. Then, having accumulated considerable money by speculating in black flesh and blood, he had gradually drifted into the cotton trade, and was now supposed to be the richest cotton broker in any of the Gulf States. He was consequently a most pronounced secessionist and an intense hater of everything that was not southern.

"You mean," said Miss Belle, spicily, "that we impulsive South Carolinians have stolen a march upon you lazy, sluggish Georgians ;—but permit me to introduce a reformed Black Republican—Mr. Lawrence Bryant, Mr. Amos Pierson."

It was vitally to my interest that Laura should conclude her interview with her father without interruption from the gentleman before me ; anxious to detain him, I joined the conversation.

"A reformed Black Republican? Why this is a curiosity!" sneered Mr. Pierson.

"I would be a curiosity if I were one," replied I, rather hotly, for the appearance of the man before me irritated me to such an extent that I was not as careful of my words as my position at the moment should have dictated.

"Ah! you are *not* a reformed Black Republican?"

"Oh, yes he is," laughed Miss Belle; "Laura has reformed him."

"Laura?" said Mr. Pierson, giving me an ugly glance, while his face grew red with some emotion the mention of my beautiful sweetheart's name brought to his mind. "Laura? What had she to do with it?"

"Oh, that you will discover in time," laughed Miss Belle. "He came here a northern man, but he has decided to remain south. He has concluded to be one of us if——"

Here I interrupted hastily: "Miss Belle imagines, because I do not contradict her southern ideas, that I have forgotten what my relatives and friends in Illinois have written to me—that it is the feeling of every one in my old home that the Union must be preserved at any cost, and in any way."

"Ah! then they would make war upon us?" laughed Mr. Pierson, showing his teeth. "Well, I am ready to eat the first northern Black Republican on the sacred southern soil of our State."

"Perhaps you had better begin with me," I returned hotly, but the conversation was here brought to an end by Miss Laura coming from the library, followed by her father, and welcoming in true southern hospitable manner the man she knew would do his utmost to frustrate what at that time I was confident from her confession must be very dear to her.

As it was growing toward evening, it was time for me to return to Columbia. Mr. Pierson, with the judge, had entered the house, while I made my adieux to Miss Belle, who then kindly turned her back upon us and allowed her sister and myself a *tête-à-tête* as I rode down the avenue.

"It's all right, Lawrence," said my *fiancée*, as soon as we were out of Miss Belle's hearing. "Papa knows I can marry no one but you, and has consented to our engagement, only stipulating that it shall not be announced, and that our marriage must be postponed until our political troubles have ceased. God grant the time may come soon."

" I echo that prayer," I whispered, as I kissed my thanks, and waving my hat, I rode laughingly and happily away, only once turning around to look at the fair girl as she stood, the setting sun illumining and making bright her face, surrounded and backgrounded by the beautiful green foliage of the avenue oaks.

"Good-by," she cried, waving her hand. "It will be all right in a month," while I reëchoed her words, and, made foolish by love, *believed them !*

CHAPTER III.

LOVE OR DUTY.

BUT during the month which I had supposed would see the political horizon clear, Mississippi, Florida, and all the Gulf States seceded, and every day made it further and further from being " all right."

The Southern Confederacy was formed, the various branches of its government completed, and company after company and regiment after regiment thronged through Columbia *en route* for Charleston, to encircle with bristling batteries and frowning guns the only fortification in South Carolina that still flaunted the flag of the United States.

This immense transportation of troops and military material made my railroad duties exceedingly arduous; consequently I had little time to visit the Peytons, though every spare moment of mine was devoted to my sweetheart, and we passed, even at that time, many happy hours together.

Laura informed me that, upon learning from her father of her contemplated matrimonial union with me, Mr. Pierson had left the next day for Savannah, having wished her—rather ironically, she thought—a happy ending to her engagement.

During this time, however, two occurrences took place

to which I gave but little heed at the moment, but which affected me very seriously shortly afterward. They were these:

One day young Caucus came into my office, and, in his excitable darky manner, said : " Mas' Bryant, dar am sev'ral officers below dat am anxious for a interview."

I ordered them to be admitted, and found that they were two members of the staff of General Beauregard who was then in command of the Confederate forces about Charleston. One of them, Stuart Bee, a Georgian and a particular friend of mine, handed me a letter tendering me a staff appointment upon the transportation corps of the Confederate army. He said they had called to ask if I did not wish to take immediate charge of the movement of the troops then being pushed forward to reinforce the Confederate soldiers already about Charleston.

I replied that I did not wish to join the Confederate army in any capacity.

"Why not ?" asked Bee. "Do you not now forward to us all the troops that pass here ?"

"Yes," I replied, "as engineer of the South Carolina Railroad, but not as a member of the Confederate army."

"Well," he replied, "you do your work in a very satisfactory manner; but I had hoped that you would accept the appointment, because it would put an immediate stop to the local prejudice that is growing up against you. For your own sake, you should make it plain that you are favorable to the Confederate cause. The report that you have refused this offer will only tend to make your position here more uncomfortable with our people who surround you."

"I am very much obliged," I replied, "for the honor tendered me, but must still refuse. I am fully sensible of the inconvenience that my declination may bring to me, but cannot reconsider the proposition. Do you know, by the bye, who was it that recommended me for the position ?"

"I believe Mr. Amos Pierson, of Savannah, who has lately accepted some large contracts for army supplies for the Confederate Government," replied my friend.

With this the two officers said good-by, leaving me to reflect that Mr. Amos Pierson, through his recommendation to General Beauregard, had succeeded in compelling me to assume a stand that in this exciting time would probably cause my social ostracism by most of my neighbors in Columbia.

Evidences of this in the next few days became apparent. My refusal to accept an office upon the staff of General Beauregard was noted by the local papers and commented upon in no flattering terms, and the cold shoulders that had been turned to me for some time past during my business and social intercourse with the citizens of the town became much more cold.

Even Laura remarked this with a sigh as she said: "What a pity, Lawrence, that you are not one of us—one who loves the South."

"As well as I do one of its maidens," laughed I, but the laugh had a rather forced and unpleasant ring in it.

The second event was the departure of young Arthur Peyton with his company to join the forces about Charleston.

The lad went off in high spirits, laughing and happy as if he were going to a picnic or a frolic, but after that a little of the coming gloom of the war descended upon his family. His father sighed more often, and Miss Laura and Miss Belle seemed to be even more southern than before in their sentiments, the latter young lady saying to me one day: "If I don't soon make a true South Carolinian of you by coaxing and by being your friend in your suit for Laura, I shall begin to try sterner measures, Mr. Lawrence Bryant."

She said this with a very sweet sixteen-year-old laugh, but I felt, notwithstanding, that there was an unpleasant tone of truth in her remark.

So things drifted on and on, always for the worse, until one day Columbia became a ferment of excitement under the news of the bombardment and capture of Fort Sumter by the Confederate forces.

From that time on I knew that there was no hope of any peaceful solution of the difficulty that had begun by the secession of South Carolina four months before.

I felt that my duty called me to the North, that my love bound me to the South, and so I lingered despite the warning of Mr. Tom Baxter, who arrived the day afterward from Georgia.

" Are you going with me, Lawrence ? " he asked.

" Going where ? "

" North, of course, while you have the chance."

" Not at present," I replied.

" Not at present ? " he echoed. " If you don't go now, you will never go. When two armies face each other in Virginia and Tennessee, it will not be so easy a matter to pass through their contending lines as it is to buy a through ticket for Washington and get north in less than two days, as I am about to do."

" Still," I replied, " I shall remain here for the present."

" Ah ! I suppose it is the young lady who still detains you ? Marry her, and take her north with you ! "

" At such a time she would not leave her father and her sister. I fear that I will lose her if I leave her, and I love her too well to give her up."

" Well, my boy," returned the sententious Tom, " if you stay here two months longer, you will not be able to leave peaceably, and you'll lose the girl anyway."

" What makes you think that ?—Laura Peyton loves me !" muttered I, in almost a tremble.

" Laura Peyton loves you *now ;* but wait till the fighting begins, and your sweetheart will very soon grow cold to a man who is not willing to risk his life for the cause *she* loves. You will not be able to stand against her prayers and entreaties ; and if you do not, you and I, my dear old chum, will perhaps meet in combat upon the battle-field. Take your last and only chance to do your duty. There'll be no half measures in this conflict. Go north and be a northern man, or remain in the South and you, *nolens volens,* will have to fight for the Confederacy."

With this Mr. Baxter proceeded on his way, but though out of my view, his remarks lingered in my mind, and had it not been for the beautiful eyes, welcoming arms, and beguiling smiles of the girl I loved, I should soon have followed Mr. Baxter north.

Thus, undecided, struggling between love and duty, I remained until *the first day of July,* 1861, drew near.

From that day the Confederate Government had decreed that all people remaining under its jurisdiction should be considered subjects of the Confederacy and not permitted to leave its borders without its permission. Such permission it was considered a military necessity not to grant, save to women, children, and persons not subject to military duty.

I was now compelled to take some definite action. After a night spent in alternate wavering between my love for my country and my love for Laura Peyton, I decided to return to the North, if possible taking her with me as my wife,—if not, hoping that she would be true to me through the few months which I thought it would probably take to settle the contest now beginning between the North and South.

Actuated by this idea, I rode out through the pretty streets of Columbia to the home of my sweetheart. It was a very calm, beautiful summer evening, but I hardly noticed it, so engrossed was I in the misery and anxiety which my resolution had brought to me.

As I rode up the avenue, a horseman rapidly passed me, apparently coming from Judge Peyton's house. He was muttering to himself in some trouble apparently greater than mine. His features were not so distorted by misery, however, that I failed to recognize in the uncertain light the face of Harry Walton. He was dressed in the uniform of a captain of the Hampton Legion, and rode by me so rapidly that I did not think he saw me, for he uttered no word of greeting, and gave me no salutation.

This was not altogether surprising, though we had been great friends a few months before, and chums at college in '55, and it was partly owing to his friendship that I had obtained my railroad position. Still, ever since the bright face of Laura Peyton had come between us, he had grown colder and colder, and his hearty shake of the hand had gradually changed to a bow, the bow to a nod, and the nod had become colder and colder, until we were now almost strangers. This was partly due to our different political sentiments, but more from his suspicion that I had found favor in the sight of the woman he loved, though as Laura's engagement to me had never been formally announced, he had by no means given up all hope of winning her hand, and his visits to her home in the last few months had been as frequent as my own.

On entering the house, I was greeted by Miss Belle, who rather cavalierly informed me that her sister would not be visible for a few minutes, but if I could waste a little of my time on her, she would tell me something that would perhaps prove to me that, notwithstanding my lukewarm southern sentiments, she was still my friend,— "though I am not going to be so much longer," she said, rather savagely.

"Well, what have you done for me?" I asked, trying to turn the conversation.

"Done for you? I have this evening, with consummate tact for a girl of my years, prevented your sweetheart's being proposed to in full form with all the romantic advantages of military uniform, broken heart, and instant departure for war and bloodshed by one Harry Walton, once attorney at law, but now captain in Wade Hampton's gallant legion. He looked so handsome in his regimentals, that I would not have given much for your chances had he ever asked Laura," remarked Miss Belle, rather sarcastically; "and if he ever comes back wounded for our glorious cause, I wouldn't give much for them any way," continued the girl, with a little laugh, partly of merriment and perhaps partly of malice.

"He didn't see her, then?"

"Oh, yes, he saw her; but he didn't have any chance to propose to her, for I took care to make the third at the parting, and didn't give him a single second for a *tête-à-tête*. Nevertheless their parting was very affectionate, and perhaps a little tender. There were tears on both sides as he bade her good-by. That is the reason she won't see you now,—red eyes are not becoming."

"And why have you done this thing for me—one whom you half dislike?" ventured I.

"Because," replied the lady, airily, "I still have hopes of you; and, until I give up in despair, am perfectly willing to be your friend; but when I do make up my mind once, definitely and forever, that you will never become one of us, that moment my good offices will leave you, and I shall do my best to assist Harry Walton in gaining the love of my sister. You see I'm an artful recruiting officer, for the C. S. A."

This conversation was now interrupted by the entrance of Laura whose white summer dress made her look to me prettier than ever—perhaps because I thought I should soon part from her.

There was a suspicion of redness in her eyes and a tearine s about her smile which indicated that her sister had not exaggerated the effect of Captain Walton's fare-well.

After a few moments' conversation, Miss Belle left the room, and I began to explain my motives and my plans to my sweetheart, once or twice interrupted by a gasp of pain and a sob that carried with it no tears.

When I had finished, she looked at me and faltered : "Lawrence, I know if you part from me now, it will be forever."

"Forever !—no, no. I'll come back for you, as sure as I stand by you now. But come with me north—-leave all this trouble behind you——"

"Leave my poor old father—my little sister—who have just now given Arthur to their country's cause—leave them ? No, no, Lawrence ; you may love me, but now you do not honor me."

"Not when I beg you to be my wife ? "

"Yes, but if I accepted—if I let myself be happy—if I deserted the South and my dear father and sister, I should despise myself. Lawrence, if you wish to retain my love, never ask me to do this mean thing again ! " This last the girl said in a haughty despair, walking up and down the room, but sometimes stopping to kiss and fondle, and at others to flash almost angry glances at me.

The scene was becoming cruel. Fortunately it was interrupted by a servant bringing in a letter addressed to Miss Laura Peyton and marked " Immediate." As she tore it open, I recognized that the handwriting was that of Harry Walton.

She glanced through it, handed it to me, and said fal-teringly : " Harry Walton asks me to marry him ; and you leave me at such a moment ? "

" What have you or I to fear from Harry Walton ? He is a gentleman," I answered.

"But there is one who is not a gentleman," she gasped. "Amos Pierson, through his business hold upon my father, still thinks to win me."

"Still thinks to win you ? A man whom you de-spise ? "

"Yes ; here are the proofs," and she handed me a bundle of letters. "I had intended to show you these some time ago, but circumstances compel me to let you read them at once. This man will not give up his hopes of my love,—will not give up his desire for my hand. Can you at such a moment, even for your political principles leave me, the woman who loves you, who has stood against the advice of the friends of her youth and the entreaties of her relatives, to be true to the promise that six months ago she gave you to be your wife? Can you desert and leave me alone for an indefinite period in a land that may perhaps become the scene of actual warfare? Can you part from me and hope to win me? Stay here, and I will love you forever; desert me, and I shall doubt the truth of your affection. Is it my love, our happiness, and your presence by my side,—or do you leave me surrounded by enemies to my affection for you, to be parted more and more from you each day by the political passions of this awful time? Will you, dare you—dare I let you—take such chances against the happiness of our lives? Do you remain in the South, or do you go north?"

Enforced by pleading eyes, clinging arms, and loving kisses from the woman he loved, what man could give an answer other than I did? "I REMAIN!"

As I left her that evening, I thought there was triumph as well as love in Laura Peyton's eyes.

The first of July, 1861, passed. I still stayed in South Carolina, was considered a citizen of the Confederacy, and became subject to Confederate military law.

CHAPTER IV.

THE EMPTY SLEEVE.

THE immense transportation now forced upon all railroads in the South, of arms, ammunition and men, to the scene of war in Virginia now occupied the most of my time.

The rest of it I gave to *her*.

In fact, almost all other social intercourse was debarred me, for the rumor had been circulated constantly, and continually gained ground in the community, that my sympathies were northern. Thus shunned by the friends and acquaintances of a few months before, I was compelled to live almost entirely by myself, and the only solace that I had was the sweet caresses and bright smiles of my *fiancée* who seemed at this time to be made even more tender than before by the recollection that for her sake I had isolated myself in a community so entirely hostile to me. These reports as to my northern sentiments were so continually and systematically spread, that I knew some one interested in annoying me circulated them. I had a faint suspicion that this was due to the efforts of Mr. Amos Pierson, who had now become one of the leading army contractors in the South, and was making a large amount of money from his operations with the Confederate Government. Consequently he had great weight and influence in its councils. This suspicion was made a certainty by another proffer of a staff appointment from General Pemberton, who had become the local commander of the district.

I again refused, and also discovered that this offer was made at Mr. Pierson's suggestion.

The local papers again published my refusal, and made longer and more violent comments upon it than before, but the Confederate Government took no action at this time as to forcing me into their service, probably knowing that my experience as a railroad engineer was of great value to them in my present location.

So the Confederacy drifted along through the varying successes and hopes and fears of the first two years of its existence.

It had become tacitly understood between my sweetheart and myself that as soon as the war was over we were to be married. I had at first hoped that this would not mean more than a year's delay, but as time wore on, the end seemed further and further in the distance. The dogged persistence of the North seemed only to become more dogged and more determined by defeat and disaster, until early in December, 1862, the battle of Fredericksburg was fought, and brought great misery to me.

The news of the success of the Confederate arms had been received by telegraph. The ladies of Columbia, and those of the men who were not in the army, were excited with the joy of triumph.

Two weeks after this battle, on Christmas Day, I had ridden out to Judge Peyton's to enjoy the only hospitality I could then find in the community. For I had no friends, though still waited upon by the faithful Caucus, who stuck to me in spite of, as he expressed it, "de an'mosity ob de South !"

Laura had received me as usual, but her sister, Miss Belle, who had by this time gradually given up all hope of making me a southerner in feeling, remarked with some asperity that she thought it was about time I showed myself to be a man, and instead of making love to young ladies, went out and fought, like other men, for them on the battle-field,—"like Major Harry Walton, for instance," for by this time death had made promotion rapid in the Confederate army, and Walton was now a major, while Arthur, their brother, but twenty-two years of age, was a captain in one of the South Carolina regiments.

The family had received no news from him, though they knew that he was in the army engaged at Fredericksburg. During the first months of the war the anxiety of the judge's family for the safety of the hope of their house had been something upon which it was fearful to look. The panting eagerness of the two girls as they read the dispatches, the suppressed apprehension with which they looked at the long lists of killed and wounded that followed every battle, made my heart bleed for them. But as engagement after engagement took place, and their brother's name never appeared in the lists of maimed or dead, such is the curious effect of habit that even they became accustomed to the suspense, and rather thought that their brother enjoyed a charmed life that could not be shortened or endangered by, as they expressed it, " Yankee bullets."

They had not received any communication from the young man since Fredericksburg, and thought it curious that he had not written to assure them of his safety. Though knowing the exigencies and demands of military life, it did not create any great anxiety in their minds, as the lists of killed and wounded, as hurriedly telegraphed from the field hospitals, had not contained the young man's name.

The judge had just come out on the veranda to smoke his after-dinner pipe, as good cigars in those days were a very rare article in the South, while corncobs and to·

bacco could be always obtained. I had accompanied him, and we were sitting down, the old gentleman talking to me about the happy Christmas days of a few years before when his son Arthur was at home—a subject on which he seemed to linger ; for the judge doted more and more upon the boy as his absence became longer. Suddenly I heard a subdued cry from Miss Belle, who was looking out of one of the upper windows over our heads, and turning around I saw a light wagon just drawing up at the steps of the house. In it upon the back seat were two Confederate officers, one of them supporting the other, who seemed in an almost fainting condition.

As the wheels stopped, he appeared to rouse himself, and said faintly, though in quite a weak voice : " Home again ! "

The next instant, with a scream, " It's Arthur's voice! " Miss Belle and the judge had run to the wagon, from which Harry Walton, with bandaged head, was supporting Arthur Peyton. They were around him in an instant with tears, caresses, and cries of joy.

Then suddenly Miss Belle shrieked out : " Arthur, where's your arm ? "

The boy gasped, " Lost at Fredericksburg," and fainted away upon his father's breast, who groaned " Great God ! it's his right arm ! " while Laura looking at him with a pale face, sobbed, " Maimed for life ! "

In a moment they had him upstairs ; I, calling for my horse to be saddled, prepared to ride into Columbia for a doctor. While this was being done, Harry Walton and I, left alone together, looked at each other on the veranda.

" You," I said, " are wounded also ? "

" Yes," replied he; " the fragment of a shell grazed my head at Fredericksburg. My hurt is slight. God knows how Laura's brother's wound will turn out ! "

We neither of us went in, to interrupt the first agony of grief that came upon the Peytons. Both Major Walton and myself considered such a scene as a sacred one.

A moment after, Miss Laura's voice was heard crying, " Get a doctor, quick ! " and Belle screamed, " Arthur's dying ! "

I sprang upon my horse, and as the judge came hurriedly upon the veranda, I shouted: " Don't fear ! I will have a doctor here as soon as horseflesh can do it," and galloped away down the avenue. An hour afterward I returned, followed by the best physician in Columbia that I could obtain,—good doctors being scarce, most of them having volunteered their services in the field.

While the physician went up to make his examination, the young ladies came downstairs, and Miss Belle, with feminine logic and philosophy, strode up to me, and with flashing eyes whispered : "It was your friends who have done this to my brother. How can you expect me ever to endure your sight again ? "

"Hush!" said Laura, coming between us. "Belle, you are unjust. Lawrence had no more to do with this than you, and has but this moment proved his friendship and sympathy by doing everything in his power to save our brother's life."

"Oh ! you love him! " cried her sister; "you love him *yet ;* but when, if my brother lives, you look at his empty sleeve, you will hate this northern man as I do." With that she walked into the house.

"Forgive her, Lawrence," said Laura, apologetically; "she is but a child. Remember her excitement, her love for her brother, and her misery at seeing him thus maimed."

"I have every consideration," I replied, "for your family in your bereavement; but think, dear Laura, in what a fearful position I am placed when every misfortune of this war is laid upon me,—when I am surrounded by enemies, and have nowhere to turn but to the friendship of you and your family."

"I will remember," said Laura; "I will *try* to remember —if I can."

As these words, ominous to my future happiness, fell from the lips of the girl I loved, the surgeon came down and made his report. With careful nursing and tender care, there was every chance for the young man's life.

"But his arm ! " almost sobbed the judge ; "his arm ! My poor maimed boy ! " and Miss Belle, after echoing her father, cried out to me, as I rode away from the house: "This is what your northern brothers have done to us, Mr. Lawrence Bryant ! "

Under these circumstances could my reflections that evening as I rode into Columbia have been pleasant ones ;

3

or my sleep that night have been the sleep of the happy and unconcerned ?

The closing catastrophe of my courtship was coming —I knew it. To reach the climax would take but a little time.

When I rode out to inquire after Arthur's health, Miss Belle received me, sometimes with scowls, sometimes with ironical remarks, that showed me that I could expect nothing from her but open animosity.

Laura attempted to palliate this and explain it, but even as she did so her manner was forced and constrained. She was not the open, light-hearted ingenuous girl who first became my sweetheart and then my affianced bride. There was evidently some secret influence upon her mind which was weaning her heart from me.

In the course of the next two months her brother had recovered sufficiently to lounge upon the veranda, the light spring air every day giving him greater and greater strength, but the empty sleeve in his uniform was a constant reminder to his sisters of what he had lost : and the helplessness of the young man with his right arm gone stimulated his family's hatred to the North, which fell upon me as its nearest representative. The old judge's cordiality of manner gradually left him, his answers to my remarks became monosyllables, and Laura herself, as she looked at that empty sleeve, seemed to grow colder and colder to me, and to show greater cordiality and warmth to Major Walton, who every day rode over to inquire how the patient progressed, and to linger all day with the young ladies after he had discovered that the patient was better, apparently charming them by his anecdotes of battle, and of dangers undertaken and endured in the defense of their beloved cause.

In such scenes I, of course, had no part, and Laura seemed to take rather a pleasure in innuendoes that taunted me for my lack of gallantry in not being a soldier, such as: " This Columbia of ours cannot interest you much, Major Walton—now that *all* the men have gone to the war "—or— " Oh! the stay-at-homes ! Were I a man like you, Mr. Bryant, I'd fight for some side ! " Such remarks she would emphasize with a haughty laugh, dwelling a little on the " Mr. Bryant," for she sometimes omitted to call me Lawrence at those times. Had I been a thorough judge of a woman's heart, or not blinded by misery ; after such speeches, I should have known that the girl's love was still entirely mine, for then she always seemed to apologize for them by her manner, and sometimes to become even more affectionate than she had ever been to me.

Thus we drifted along, until one day the sword of Damocles, which had hung over our engagement by so fragile a hair, descended and severed, apparently, the love that had bound us together.

It was a slight incident that brought about the crisis.

I had been talking with Arthur, who was now convalescent, but of course entirely disabled for active military service. The young man, who had all through this affair been very cordial and friendly to me, was saying that he would like, as soon as he was a little stronger, to obtain employment on the railroad of which I was one of the officers, remarking : "You, Bryant, know that now I've got to use my brains for a living, not my hands." As he said this, the young fellow gazed at his empty sleeve, and a little spasm of agony ran over his face ; then, trying to conjure up a grin, he cried : " Pshaw ! If I only had left the *feeling* of it when I lost it !—but though it's buried up at Fredericksburg, it ached all night. That cold Virginia ground must have given it the rheumatism."

Feeling for the boy's helplessness, I remarked : " You'll soon grow resigned to your loss, Arthur."

" Perhaps he would," said Miss Belle, who had been listening to us, clad in a dark homespun dress, for the blockade by this time was beginning to tell upon the ladies' costumes down south, " if he had another man to take his place." Then she whispered to me : " Major Walton goes to the front again to-day. This time I did not interrupt his *tête-à-tête* with Laura—and the result—see ! "

She pointed through a vista of shrubbery, and as I looked I gave a start. Walton was evidently taking leave of my sweetheart, and this time he seemed in great spirits as he mounted his horse.

What man who loves is not jealous sometimes ? Walton left in despair the last time—now he seemed radiant. Had Laura given him hope ?

Thus working myself into a fit of rage, I walked down the avenue toward my *fiancée*, who was just waving a very gracious adieu to the dashing major.

I can see her now as she looked then, every graceful curve in her girlish figure standing out in full relief against the clear blue of the April sky ; for the scarcity of cloth of all kinds in the South at that time compelled even the women of the wealthiest classes to dress as economically as possible, and Laura's frock of some home-made jean or cotton was entirely without ornamental fluff or flounce to destroy the beauty of her exquisite form, that combined the graces of the girl with the grander beauties of womanhood.

There she stood clad in homespun, a few wild flowers upon the bosom of her dress, a slight flush upon her face, that gradually became paler as she saw the excited agony in mine.

" You were bidding Major Walton good-by—judging by his look, I should presume the parting had been a tender one," I said, with a slight sneer, for these long months of trouble had come upon me all at once to make me passionate and hasty.

" You—you take a very curious tone to me to-day, Lawrence," murmured the girl, growing slightly paler.

" Not more curious than the tones you have taken to me ever since your brother returned," answered I, hotly.

This was by no means diplomatic on my part, as it made Laura remember Arthur's sufferings and loss, that had gradually made her colder to me as a northern man.

The color came back in a rush to her cheeks. " You do well, Mr. Bryant, to remind me of what has come to me and mine from the hands of your friends," she said, haughtily. " You have made me at last remember what my love for you made me forget—that I am a southern girl."

Her answer told me of my mistake, but I was desperately jealous, and sneered : " That remembrance was, I presume, assisted by Major Walton ! "

" It was ! "

" Ah ! "

" It was assisted by every southern man I saw fighting for his country—Harry Walton among the rest," she returned, haughtily. Then, falteringly, " Lawrence, I have loved—God knows how I've loved—and hoped day by day to win you, through your love of me, to our cause and our side—that *my* country would be *your* country—but now,"—here she gasped and staggered a little, and then, as if filled with some mighty idea that gave her courage, she drew herself up, and with a calmness, perhaps of despair, uttered : " But now you will not become one of us in love for the South—your kindred will never be my kindred, and at such a time it is not right that a southern girl should wed an enemy of her country ! "

" You would not say such words if you had ever loved me ! "cried I, in agony, for I knew my sweetheart was going to be mine no more.

" Ever loved you ? " she faltered. " Ever loved you ? What passion do you call it that makes a girl endure the jeers of her friends and scoffs of her kindred to cling to the man they hate and despise ? Is not that devotion ? Is not that true love ? That is what for two years I have given to you, Lawrence Bryant. That is what this ring has cost me ! " And as she said this, she took my engagement ring off her finger.

" My God ! You are going to leave me ! " I cried.

" Yes. It has come at last, Lawrence—at last ! This ring is mine no longer ! " and she held it out to me, and I trembled, for I knew that Laura Peyton, the girl I still loved, was my sweetheart no more. The next moment the ring dropped from her faltering hand upon the grass, and she fell fainting into Miss Belle's arms, who shrieked out at me :

" You've broken my sister's heart ! I'll make you fight on *one side or the other* for this, you Yankee ! " And the girl shook her fist at me, a perfect picture of rage.

As I rode away, I took my last look at the house in which I left so many pleasant memories. The old judge was smoking on the veranda ; the oaks were as green and beautiful as ever, but the love—the love of the girl I loved—that had left me, and the place looked as desolate as the war had made my heart.

BOOK II.

How I Fled from Her.

CHAPTER V.

A CONFEDERATE DETECTIVE.

My love was lost to me. What was there to hold me to this place, an alien, surrounded by enemies? I determined to leave South Carolina. I remembered Miss Belle's threat. If I was to fight I would fight for the cause that I loved. I resolved to go north through the Confederate lines—at this time a very difficult matter, though four routes were open to me. One was to get to Wilmington, or some other port, the resort of blockade-runners, and so to Nassau ; another, by way of Suffolk and Norfolk to the Union lines in Virginia ; a third, to go to the coast of South Carolina, and escape by boat to some Union war ship off the coast or to the Federal troops garrisoning Hilton Head ; the fourth was through western North Carolina and eastern Tennessee. This latter was very hazardous, as there were a great many bushwhackers and guerillas all along the route. The one to the near sea-coast was not so long, but was well guarded by South Carolinians, who were so entirely devoted to the southern cause, that I could find no Union sympathizers to help me on my way, although in the last few months I had known of men escaping by this route.

After careful deliberation, I determined to go by way of Suffolk and Norfolk, as my connection with railroads would give me passes and ticket accommodations, perhaps, where other people could not get them. Beside this, I would obtain aid from a secret organization of Union men in North Carolina.

I knew I had no time to lose, and made my arrangements hurriedly. Once only did I hesitate in my course, and that was the day after my last interview with Laura, at "The Oaks." I was walking down the main street of Columbia, busied with some of my preparations for departure that I was compelled to make in the most guarded, careful, and surreptitious manner, when two young ladies passed me on horseback. A glance showed me that they were the Misses Peyton. Miss Belle gave me a haughty, unrecognizing glance. Laura looked at me, seemingly about to speak, then faltered, and, apparently urged by her sister, rode on. A single word to me, from her, I believe, even at that moment, would have held me in South Carolina. With my heart in my eyes, I looked after the girl I loved as she rode away. Twice Laura seemed to hesitate as if she would turn back, each time opposed by her sister. Once she nearly made the movement, but Miss Belle seized her bridle and turned her horse once more away from me, apparently saying a few hurried words to her. As she did so, I saw Laura's graceful form clad in its gray, homespun habit, sway in the saddle ; but after that she never attempted to gaze back or turn again. I staggered away to my office and there found a document that hurried my arrangements for departure.

Had I known it, however, I would have found that before my sweetheart had ridden a quarter of a mile she had, despite her sister's tears, entreaties, and rage, deliberately returned along the street, trying in vain to find me, to tell me the words for which I longed.

The document I gazed at was an official order from the general commanding the district to report for active service in the Confederate army at Charleston within seven days.

Accompanying the command was a letter from my friend Bee, on General Beauregard's staff, which ran as follows :

"HEADQUARTERS DEPARTMENT S. C., GA., AND FLA., }
CHARLESTON, *April* 1, 1863. }

"MY DEAR BRYANT : I have just learned the news that you are to be ordered to take active service with the Confederacy. As to the legality of this order, there can, of course, be no doubt, you having remained two years within our borders after the time allowed for the departure of aliens. You have probably been permitted to remain in your position as engineer of the South Carolina Railroad because the Confederacy needed your services as such. Now, however, the 'powers that be' have decided that you become one of us. I advise you to make no opposition, as it will only entail trouble and danger upon you. Come to Charleston quietly, and if in my power, I will see that you get a staff appointment,—something that will not compel you to absolutely use your arms against the people I have a strong suspicion you regard as your brothers. A word to the wise is sufficient, as I know everything will be done to compel your complete compliance with the order that has been sent you,—your friend, Mr. Amos Pierson, having taken an apparently active interest in this matter and an army contractor being at present a power in the South. Your well-wisher,

"STUART BEE."

The effect of this was simply to hasten my departure from Columbia. I completed my preparations, and next morning, the 3d day of April, 1863, boarded a train on the Charleston, Columbia and Augusta Railroad for Graham, N. C., at which point I expected to meet a friend who would advise me as to the best way to reach Suffolk.

In these preparations I was necessarily compelled to make a confidant of my valet, the red-headed Caucus. This disclosure I made after pledging him to secrecy very privately in my office the night before I left. Then Caucus surprised me.

I had supposed him devoted, body and soul, to his masters in the South, but he burst out: " Oh, 'fore de Lord, Massa Bryant, if I could get north wid you ! "

" Go with me ? "

" Yes. I's longin' to hear de Yankee gunboats fire, dat means freedom for dis darky."

" Why, I had supposed that you loved the Peytons too well to wish ever to leave their service."

" Yas, I lub de Peytons ; dey has been mighty kind to me ; but I lub habin' my own way, and doin' nothin' when I choose to bettar. Dar's white blood in me, Massa Bryant ; look at my head ! De redness of it means dat I's a spirit dat 'll fight for bossin' myself. I's named Caucus cause I's Caucussion ! "

" It is impossible for me to take you with me. I could never get you through to the Union lines."

" Don't I know dat ? " returned Caucus. " Haven't I thought of dat ! Wouldn't I have gone myself long ago if I had reckoned I could fotch dar ! Why is you goin', Massa Bryant ? Why you not want de Peytons to know ?

Has de young missus gwine and gib you de shake?
Always reckon she wah powerful gwine on you, sah.
Mighty sorry to see you leab, sah."

Caucus would have run on for half the night lamenting
my departure, and expressing astonishment and wonder,
had not I cut him short by handing him a letter to the
railroad company resigning my office in their employ, and
charging him as he loved my personal safety not to deliver
it to the corporation *until one week* from the time of my
departure.

I then spent the remainder of the night completing my
preparations. I had gradually, during the last few months,
exchanged all the Confederate money I had for U. S.
greenbacks, trading these little by little, as time and oc-
casion permitted, with the Federal prisoners in Columbia.
As Confederate money had greatly depreciated, and I had
now over one thousand dollars in greenbacks, I took
five hundred of this sum, considering that it would be
sufficient to carry me north. The rest I inclosed in a
short note to Laura, telling her that I knew from the
certain poverty coming to all in South Carolina that some
day or other this money would be of service to her, begging her to accept it as a loan from one who would never
cease to wish to be her friend, and who would never forget that she was the only woman he had loved—who still
thought her to be the only woman he would ever love.
This missive I charged young Caucus to give to Miss
Peyton on the same day he delivered my resignation to
the railroad company, and for no cause whatsoever to
deliver either of the messages before the time I had instructed him.

When I set out on my journey I had with me a
Colt's revolver and cartridges, my money, the best suit
of clothes I possessed, and a few cherished mementoes
of the girl I still loved but left behind me. I had already
sent a message to a friend of mine in North Carolina
who was a Union man ; besides this the bond of masonic
fellowship being also between us, I knew that he would
never betray me.

I had no sooner boarded the cars than a great difficulty
confronted me. My long connection with a leading
southern railway made me known to nearly all brakemen,
conductors, and engineers upon the different roads over

which I traveled, and consequently forbade any attempt at traveling under an assumed name unless I could thoroughly disguise myself. To all inquiries as to my destination I replied that I was going on railroad business to North Carolina and Virginia. There were several Confederate officers on the train, traveling to join their various commands, who seemed to look with suspicion upon any one dressed in citizen's clothes, but after seeing me recognized by the conductor as one of the officers of the South Carolina Railroad, their suspicions were lulled. The same effect was also produced upon two or three army detectives that were upon the train looking out for deserters and stragglers from the Confederate ranks.

Travel at that time in the South was by no means pleasant, as the railroads were gradually getting into a very dilapidated and unsafe condition from the inability of their authorities to provide them with either new iron or rolling stock,—nearly all the iron in the Confederacy being seized by the Confederate Government for the manufacture of cannon and other war material.

I determined that the railroad business that carried me away from Columbia should be the pursuit of some new rails for the South Carolina Railroad.

This point decided, I sat down in the car and ruminated in that kind of stunned daze that comes upon every man after one of those great earthquakes of life that tear up and destroy the desires, aims, and social topography of existence. I was flying from the woman who had been for three years the one object of my thoughts by day, my dreams by night ; not because I did not love her, but because I feared that if I stayed within reach of her, she would allure me to the cause I hated, and make me, like herself, ready to fight the people whom I loved.

At this moment I presume I must have given a sigh or groan, or something of the kind, for a peculiar, twangy, nasal North Carolina voice broke in on my reverie, saying : " You don't look 'ticular spunky this morning, Mr. Bryant. Can't you move your head a little so I can git a square spit through the keer window ? "

I moved my head, and recognized Pete Bassett, a government detective, who had been about our railroad yards for the last few weeks looking after the Federal prisoners of war that were at this time arriving in large numbers from the North for confinement in the stockade near the town.

Mr. Bassett seemed inclined to be chatty. Unheeding my apparent disinclination for conversation, he insisted on telling me of the various escaped Federal prisoners he had assisted in recapturing, punctuating his anecdotes by squirts of tobacco juice that he delivered with the precision of a marksman at the telegraph poles that we ran past.

He invited me to drink at every station. Do what I could he seemed to be at my elbow. His very cordiality seemed to me suspicious. I became convinced that for some reason or other his gray eyes, reddened by bad whisky, were always on me, and that he had a particular interest in my movements. I determined to test this.

At the next stopping place I knew that the train ran up the track to a water tank and then returned to the station before proceeding on its way.

I jumped off the cars as we ran slowly past the place, and to my disgust Bassett sprang off also.

"What did you bolt the train for, Mr. Bryant?" he asked.

"Why, to stretch my legs," I replied. "It's only going for water and 'll be back in five minutes. What made you jump it also?"

"Wall—for—for about the same objict," he muttered. "You see I reckoned you knew the customs of your road, and wouldn't be after being left yourself. I calculated your lead was a good one to follow.—Have another pull at my corn juice?"

"No, thank you!" remarked I.

A few moments afterward the train returned, but I boarded it with a sinking heart. I knew Pete Bassett, one of the coolest sleuth-hounds in the Confederacy, was on my trail—that my attempt to gain the Union lines was being shadowed.

After running off the track once, and being detained several hours, we arrived at Charlotte, where I had to wait two hours before resuming my journey.

In this place I expected to meet no one to help me; but at Graham I anticipated seeing my Union friend.

I therefore acted in such a manner at Charlotte, as would throw Bassett off his guard at Graham.

Immediately on my arriving in Charlotte I went about looking apparently for a friend at the depot, though I expected to meet no one. I then wandered about the town, up one street and down another, all the time conscious that I was dogged by Mr. Bassett. After doing this apparently without an object, which was exactly what I would in Graham a few hours after *with* an object, I returned to the hotel, casually met my pursuer, and asked him to drink with me, saying I'd been killing time looking about the town, but had not seen a soul I knew, all the men being at the war, and I not much of a hand at making friends with ladies.

I then boarded the train, Mr. Bassett accompanying me, and reached Graham at three o'clock in the afternoon.

Here, telling Bassett I would lay over for the night, being tired of the continual jolting of the train on the bad track, I wandered about the railroad depot. Goodshaw, the Union friend of mine, was there to meet me, but I passed him with an unknowing glance and a muttered " To-night."

He in these suspicious times being of quick wit, said nothing, but boarded the train as if looking for the arrival of some one else.

I was sure Bassett suspected nothing, and my wandering about Charlotte had made him careless in his watch on me.

After a little time in the depot, I went to the hotel, deposited my carpet-bag there, took an apparently aimless walk about the village, as I had done in Charlotte, taking care to pass the house of George Goodshaw, and note that the window blinds were tied with red, white and blue cords—a signal among the Union men of that part of North Carolina that the house could be visited in safety.

Satisfied in this, I continued my ramble, finally reaching the hotel, taking supper with Mr. Bassett, and afterward playing euchre with him for the drinks. Losing most of the games, I got disgusted at my hard luck and went to bed, Bassett doing the same.

Half an hour afterward I sneaked from my room in the hotel. As I opened the door I heard a noise like the banging of a boot a little farther along the passage way in the chamber I knew to be occupied by Bassett, and on looking, by the dim light of the hall, found a string running from the knob of my door in that direction. In a flash I knew the detective was on the alert. I ran down the stairs as quietly but as rapidly as possible, and in a moment was in the open air. I could hear Bassett's feet on the stairs in pursuit. As I did so, the whistle of an incoming train sounded in the still night air. I knew the time-table of the road. It was the night express bound north.

As if by instinct I turned and ran toward the depot, and as I ran I thought Bassett's steps sounded but fifty yards behind mine. I would make him think I took that train ; if he boarded it, I should then be free to consult with my friend unmolested. I gained the depot, and took care that he saw me enter it, then jumped on the platform of one of the cars, passed through it, descended leisurely on the other side, and strolled into the darkness. I remained in the gloom of an old woodshed, and could discern by the dim light of the station Bassett searching for me on the train. The whistle blew, the wheels revolved, and the detective, sure that I was on it, rolled off northward to Raleigh. I was alone in Graham.

CHAPTER VI.

THE PROVOST MARSHAL.

A few minutes afterward I found myself at Goodshaw's grasping his hospitable hand. His cheery voice said : "Well, getting out of the woods at last, Bryant? I would do the same, but I have a family, and that ties me here."

We consulted eagerly as to the best routes to take for my escape. The eastern portion of the State was considered dangerous on account of guerilla warfare. I might make my way either by the Cape Fear or Neuse river in a boat, to the Federal war-ships. Some had escaped that way guided by negroes in the night from one point of the river to another, the blacks always proving entirely reliable guides, and no instance being known of

their ever having betrayed any Union men who had trusted
in them.   But to this route there was a serious objection
because the terminal points were too far from the Federal
lines.   If I reached Newberne by the coast I would then
have to travel north through dismal swamps, before
reaching the Federal gunboats, and the people about this
portion of the country were so entirely in sympathy with
the Confederate cause, that from them I could expect no
aid.

Upon hearing of the difficulties attending a journey
upon these routes, I determined to attempt to make my
way out of the Confederate lines by Suffolk and Norfolk,
going *via* Weldon on the Seaboard and Roanoke Railroad.   Then I explained to Goodshaw the pursuit of
Bassett.   He looked very serious at this, but said : " The
detective is one train ahead of you. Let us hope that
he will go beyond the point at which you must leave the
railroad."

Next morning, as I paid my hotel bill, the proprietor
asked me if I knew the name of the thief who had run
away in the night without paying his bill.

The train soon took me to Raleigh, where I received
further assistance from another friend.   Fortunately this
gentleman was on very good terms with the provost marshal at Raleigh, and introduced me to him, and he, recog-
nizing me as one of the officers of the South Carolina
Railway, kindly gave me a pass to Richmond, I telling
him I was going there to attempt to induce the Confederate Government to permit us to have some new rails, in
order to repair our road, which was now in quite an unser-
viceable condition.

As this was almost a military duty for the service of
the Confederacy, I not only got a passport, but was invited
by the provost marshal to dinner.

As every day added to the danger of my being' suspected and arrested, because the moment I did not report
at Charleston according to orders from the Confederate Government, I would be considered as a deserter, I
declined the provost marshal's dinner, and arrived at
Goldsboro next morning, Monday.   This place was under
strict martial law.

I found out that a man in citizen's costume was a very
rare sight, in this part of the Confederacy, and that he was

always regarded with more or less suspicion. Many officers would immediately demand his passport. Fortunately mine was of the right kind.

Here, while in the depot preparatory to taking the train
for Weldon, two curious incidents took place that changed
the whole form of my attempt to escape.

I had hardly been in the depot a moment before, to
my dismay, I met my friend Mr. Bassett.

He gave me a very surly scowl and growled, " I was
coming back looking for you. That was a mighty mean
trick you played on me at Graham t'other night. I
have been 'way up to Weldon, reckoning you was on the
keers with me."

" Trick ? " replied I. " What trick ? I should rather
think it was a trick that you played on the hotel-keeper,
running off in the middle of the night and not paying
your board bill. He is looking for you, also."

" That kind of talk won't do," said Bassett, savagely.
" I have got instructions to look out for you, and I have
a mind to arrest you at once ! "

The only way with this man was to dominate and crush
him.

My passport made me bold. I said : " Arrest me if
you dare ! You will soon find yourself in jail if you try
it. Have you got a warrant ? "

" No," he said, " but I have got *instructions !* "

" Very well," replied I. " You disturb me in my business, and I will have you pulled over the coals at Richmond in a way that will astonish you. Look at this passport ! "

I poked in his face the one issued by the provost
marshal at Raleigh. The sight of it made him gasp with
astonishment.

" Do you see this ? " said I. " This is a permit to go
to Richmond on *military business of importance to the
Confederate Government !* You dare to disturb me, and I
don't know what a court-martial will do with you ! "

" No," he muttered, " I would not dare lay a hand on
the man with that passport," for this " business of importance to the Confederate Government " cowed and astonished him. " But all the same," said he, " I will go to
Richmond with you to see that you execute it ! Business of importance to the Confederate Government ? "

muttered he, moving away. " Don't forgit, I'll be on the train with you, Mr. Bryant, but as she won't roll out for about fifteen minutes, I'll fill my bottle with corn juice for the journey." With that Bassett walked off through the depot, about as completely crushed a detective as I ever saw.

I was meditating upon Mr. Bassett's kindness about going to Richmond with me, to be sure that I executed that " business of importance to the Confederate Government," when the telegraph clerk hurriedly cried out very excitedly to the people in the depot : " Great news from Longstreet ! He has driven the Yanks back on Norfolk ! "

The remarks I heard from the people about me convinced me that I would have little chance of escaping from Suffolk county into the Federal lines. Longstreet had so advanced his lines by driving the Union troops back, that my journey would be considerably lengthened and its dangers and difficulties materially heightened. With Mr. Bassett waiting to board the same train I did, I felt that, should I leave the cars at Weldon, as I intended, he would follow me. Under these circumstances, without a passport through Longstreet's lines, my escape would be impossible.

As I meditated, a special train bound south ran suddenly into the station. At all events, I must put Mr. Bassett off my track. The train for the south attracted my attention. Bassett, I knew, had made up his mind I was going north. A sudden thought, almost an inspiration, flashed through my brain. The conductor of the train for the south cried " All aboard ! "

Its wheels commenced to re olve, I hurriedly crossed the platform, and mounted the last of its moving cars. We ran out of the station. I felt certain I had accomplished my object. The detective was left behind me. With a sigh of relief I passed into one of the cars, which was poorly furnished, worn out and dilapidated, as were all railroad cars in the Confederacy at that time. There was a heterogeneous mass of people in this car, among them three or four red-faced men who were talking loudly, and smoking such cigars as I had not seen for years—evidently genuine Havanas.

They were apparently seafaring men. I listened to

their conversation, and discovered that they were captains of blockade-runners whose vessels were at Wilmington, and who had run up to Richmond on a pleasure trip while their ships were discharging their cargoes and taking in cotton. One of them, a burly, jovial, good-natured Briton, called by his companions Captain Samson, was telling some anecdotes connected with his profession that moved his listeners to shrieks of laughter. Even with the excitement and peculiar difficulties of my situation about me, one of them has to this day impressed itself upon my mind.

"You see," remarked Samson, "the Yankee government had to get so many new officers and sailors into its service to keep up this blockade that is making our fortunes, that a number of old merchant captains received appointments as lieutenants and masters in the regular United States Navy,—among them an absent-minded New England skipper named Eph Starbuck, who had been the last twenty years captain of the *Mary Jane*, a Boston coaster that ran regularly to Charleston, South Carolina. He was placed as lieutenant on board a gun-boat bound to that port because he was supposed to know every channel and outlet from Charleston as well as a local pilot.

"Well, one night he was officer of the watch on his little gun-boat looking out for blockade-runners, when suddenly he heard a hail from another Federal cruiser—'Ship ahoy!'

"'Ahoy, there!' answered Starbuck.

"'What ship is that?'

"'*Mary Jane* for Charleston, with general merchandise!' growled Starbuck from force of habit.

"The next minute his gun-boat was boarded and captured by the Federal cruiser, who of course thought she was a blockade-runner! It is rumored that Starbuck who was half asleep at the time had forgotten all about the war, and as his Federal friends boarded him, yelled out, 'Pirates!'"

A moment after, the entrance of the conductor stopped my laughter, and forced my mind to my own situation. I did not know even where the train was bound—I must find that out immediately, I was going away from Richmond; consequently my passport was now useless.

4

"You are bound for your vessel, I suppose," I said, touching the arm of the red-faced Briton.

"Yes, sir, to Wilmington. We go down the river to-day." Then I knew the train must be for Wilmington. The conductor was rapidly approaching me. I knew that in the absence of a ticket which I had failed to purchase, he would demand a passport. I had none and I felt that I could not obtain one.

As he approached me, with an effrontery born of the desperate nature of my situation I said : "Conductor, can you give me the directions to the provost marshal's office at Wilmington ?"

"Certainly," he replied giving me the address.

"Thank you," said I. "Can't you go with me and show me the place when the train gets there, as I have never been in the city before ?"

"Of course I can," said the conductor. "Your passport ?"

"I haven't got any. You can go with me to the provost marshal's office. I left hurriedly on immediate business. I have to go to Nassau to obtain iron for the railroad of which I am engineer. Here is my card."

"Ah, Mr. Bryant, I know you very well by reputation," replied the conductor, "and I believe I have passed over your line under a pass signed by you."

I tendered him my fare.

"Oh, no. Not from a railroad man in your position."

I remarked that I had not had time to obtain a passport, as it was necessary for us to have the iron at once.

"Yes, the rails are in bad condition. I wish you could buy some for our road while you are getting your own. Gracious ! that was a thundering jolt !" remarked the conductor as we rolled over a dilapidated rail.

This official's apparent knowledge of me seemed to dispel any suspicion which my civilian dress had caused among the passengers of the train.

I entered into conversation with the captains of the blockade-runners, and soon obtained all the information that I wished with regard to taking passage for Nassau.

"You had better come on my boat, the *Dart*," said Samson. "We leave to-day at two. I have made three successful in-and-out trips already, so you are pretty certain of not being captured."

"No," I replied, "I shall hardly be able to leave immediately."

But at that very moment my mind was made up, whether he knew it or not, to be a passenger on Captain Samson's steamer. The details I received with regard to passengers upon a blockade-runner were all very satisfactory, except this one, which made a great impression on me at the time, and a much stronger one soon afterward. Each vessel, before she was permitted to go down the river, was smoked and poled for stowaways fleeing from Confederate jurisdiction or military service. This operation was explained to me at length, and was as follows : The blockade-runners being invariably loaded with cotton, stowaways were compelled to conceal themselves among the bales. To prevent this, all interstices between the bales upon the upper deck were thoroughly explored by long, sharp poles, so that if the fugitive had any feelings whatever his cries generally made his presence known to the Confederate soldiers ; but as the poling was not always as successful in the hold of the vessel, after the cotton had been probed as well as it was possible to do it, the hatches of the boat were shut down and the hold was thoroughly fumigated by dense smoke from burning rosin, which, as the captain remarked, if it didn't bring out the skulker, generally killed him.

"I brought two corpses into Nassau last time," remarked the skipper, sententiously, with a jovial, kindhearted laugh that sent a shudder through me.

The distance between Goldsboro and Wilmington by rail in those days was about seventy miles ; but such was the wretched state of the road-bed that our train took nearly five hours to make the run. In fact, a hand-car could have almost made the trip in the same time. I had ample evidence of the fact a little later.

Arrived in Wilmington, I stepped off the cars before they had ceased their motion, and sheltering myself behind one of the numerous cotton bales piled up by the side of the railroad track, scanned the faces of the passengers as they descended from the train. After close scrutiny I gave a sigh of relief. I was now entirely sure that Bassett was separated from me for the present.

I had determined upon a plan while on my journey to Wilmington. I got hold of the conductor and he took me to the provost marshal's office. I asked to see the officer in command, and after a few moments was shown in to that gentleman. I found him to be a pale, sallow captain of Louisiana volunteers, with piercing black eyes, a jet black moustache and a rather comical, but decidedly sharp smile. He had lost a leg at Malvern Hill, was dressed in fatigue Confederate uniform and was smoking an excellent Havana cigar which had been presented to him by some of his friends, the captains of blockade-runners, who found it well to be on good terms with the provost marshal of the port to which their vessels ran. He answered to the name of Captain Duquesne, and his smile might be said to be at high tide when I came in. He was hurriedly giving directions to a sergeant in attendance as to the disposal of three or four refugees that had been discovered on board a blockade-runner that day by the unpleasant yet effective process called " probing and smoking."

This was by no means reassuring to me, but I opened my business with as off-hand and take-it-for-granted a manner as possible.

"I have come," said I, " as chief engineer of the South Carolina Railway to obtain from you a pass to leave the Confederacy and visit Nassau upon a blockade-runner in order to make a contract with English capitalists to furnish railroad iron for the road of which I am an officer."

"Your name?" asked the captain.

I presented my card, fortunately having one or two yet in my possession.

"Ah, Mr. Bryant," he said smiling, "permit me to introduce myself. Captain Duquesne, tenth Louisiana Volunteers, C. S. A., Acting Provost Marshal, Wilmington, N. C., and to present you with a cigar."

I accepted the cigar, and, ye gods ! how I enjoyed it !— the first genuine Havana I had smoked for over two years.

"You have a pass, I presume, Mr. Bryant?" said the captain between the whiffs of his Cabaña.

I bowed and presented mine.

" Ah," he remarked, looking rather suspicious ; " this is to Richmond, not Wilmington."

" I was on my way to Richmond," I replied, " but

found when I reached Goldsboro that it would be impossible to obtain railroad iron in Richmond, as the Confederate authorities need every scrap in their possession for war purposes. Consequently I took the other and only plan. The railroad I represent has been of the greatest use to the Confederacy in forwarding supplies, war material, and men for the government at Richmond. You know that !"

" Certainly ! "

" It has not had a new rail laid down upon it for over two years. If new iron is not placed upon some portions of its road-bed it will be unable to perform the work your government requires of it. It is absolutely necessary that we should have at least three thousand tons of new rails almost immediately. The only hope I have of obtaining them is by buying them in England, and for that purpose it is necessary for me, in order to get them quickly, to proceed at once to Nassau."

" How will you buy them in England?" asked the captain.

" The road I represent has accumulated a large amount of cotton for that purpose, which it will ship out of the Confederacy by blockade-runners to pay for the iron forwarded to us from England."

" Ah !" said the captain, a smile illuminating his countenance as he did a little rapid figuring upon a piece of coarse brown paper in front of him, " iron rails would be worth—about fifty cents per pound laid down in Wilmington by blockade-runners, three thousand tons would cost one million five hundred thousand dollars. For this you would have to pay in cotton, worth on the wharves at Wilmington five cents per pound, which would be about thirty million pounds—sixty thousand bales. What a cursed lot of cotton your railroad must have, and what an awful lot of blockade-runners it will require to carry it out !"

" We haven't quite that much on hand," replied I, " but will have it by the time it is necessary to make deliveries. I shall contract, however, for such iron as we can pay for. Even one thousand tons of new rails would be of some advantage to us."

" Certainly, but not a great deal, for so long a track as yours, judging by the state of the road-beds about here.

You see, my dear Mr. Bryant, I was educated at West Point, and graduated into the engineers." Here he gave me another smile.

I cursed my luck at having run against an engineer officer as provost marshal.

" You won't grant me the pass ? " I asked.

" I will telegraph to the authorities at Columbia, and if your journey is approved, will issue the pass to-morrow. Take another cigar, and enjoy Wilmington," and Duquesne bowed me out of his office. Without waiting to argue further upon the matter, I immediately left, knowing I was doomed the minute a telegraphic reply from Columbia reached the provost marshal. My heart felt as heavy as if the irons were even now upon my wrists. At the most I had but three or four hours' liberty.

I wandered about in an aimless way, hardly knowing where I went. By some fatality I found myself at the railroad depot gazing in a dreamy manner at the freight trains, that were bringing in load after load of cotton. I had done this but a few moments, when I gave a start ; my mind, roused by an electric shock, resumed its functions.

The electric shock was a hand-car coming with all its speed into the station, propelled by eight stalwart negroes reeking with perspiration, and on that car, calmly chewing his usual cud of tobacco, Mr. Peter Bassett. Fortunately he did not see me. I sneaked away among the cotton-bales, and knew that I had hardly fifteen minutes more of freedom. The moment the detective reported to the provost marshal, orders would be issued for my arrest.

CHAPTER VII.

THE BLOCKADE-RUNNER.

As I hurried from the depot, my eyes fell upon the railroad clock. Its hands made the time fifteen minutes of two.

A sudden thought flashed through my mind. Captain Samson, the burly British commander of the *Dart*, had said his vessel would leave at two o'clock in the day, and drop down the river to Fort Fisher, from there that evening to make the attempt to run through the Federal blockading squadron. I determined to take the chance of leaving the Confederacy without a pass on the *Dart*. I hurried to the levee, which was probably at that time the busiest point in the whole Southern States. Numerous blockade-runners were discharging cargoes of miscellaneous manufactures, guns, ammunition and material of war for the Confederacy, while others were being loaded to their gunwales with bale upon bale of cotton, to give labor to the starving spinners of Manchester. The more a boat looked like a mountain of cotton, the nearer she was ready to sail.

I saw a sharp, rakish-looking craft of about four hundred tons, of a dull, leaden color from the top of her low smoke-stack to her water line, her deck piled with at least two tiers of cotton bales, and read upon her stern "*Dart*."

A number of negro stevedores were employed putting on board a few extra bales that were generally considered the perquisites of the officers of the ship. The boat was evidently almost ready to leave. One of these negro stevedores came around a large pile of cotton bales, evidently in search of something. It was his pipe which he had forgotten.

As he picked up the pipe, I touched him on the shoulder and held out a one-hundred-dollar greenback. The darkey's eyes rolled, his lips watered, for one hundred dollars in greenbacks meant a great deal more than one thousand in Confederate money.

I said : "Conceal me on board that vessel, and this is yours."

The darkey, who was a man of herculean build, shook his head, and said : "I'd like de hundred, Massa, but de job ain't possible."

He and a companion who had joined him stooped to lift another bale of cotton, when, with an inspiration born of desperation, I whispered, "The job is possible ! Put me inside of that bale ; then you can carry me on board."

"Golly ! " said the first darkey, and "Holy Moses ! " said the second.

" One hundred dollars, and put me in that bale ! " repeated I.

" You'se got to make it two fifties, massa, and we'll do it. We won't neber dar change a hundred-dollar bill. Dat throw 'spicion on us to once."

I hurriedly sought in my pocket-book and produced the required denominations, while with a celerity that astonished me the two stevedores ripped up the bale of cotton, and tore out enough of it to permit my concealment. Giving them the money, I found myself nearly smothered in the white fleece that gave to the South the sinews of war with which it fought so desperately for four years.

Whispering to me that they would stow the bale in a place from which I could get out, the two negroes picked me up and after a few moments' rapid motion, I judged from the bale being put down again that I was on board the *Dart*. Before leaving me, one of the darkeys cut the bands that confined the bale and pulled me out of it.

I found myself in a space not over a foot high between the top of the cargo in the hold and the lower deck. An angle made by a beam left space enough between the cargo and the ship to receive my body. Into this I was unceremoniously hustled by the stevedore, who made me very uncomfortable by this remark as he departed :

" Seems to me dis beam may sabe you from de probin' an' pokin', but, fo' de Lord, when it comes to de smokin', I pities you Massa Runaway."

I had not much time to meditate upon the ominous significance of the stevedore's words, for I soon heard the throbbing of the engine and the revolutions of the twin screws by which the vessel was propelled, and knew that she must be under way. My heart gave a jump of joy. I had escaped the poking and smoking !

The vessel had hardly been in motion a quarter of an hour, when I could hear the captain replying to a hail, apparently from a patrol boat. The engines stopped, and a minute after Samson's hearty English voice exclaimed : " So you have come on board, as usual, to do your searching and smoking ? This is the third successful trip I have made, and you never omit it, though you have not found any contrabands on board yet."

At this remark, my spirits, which had been buoyant ever since the vessel left Wilmington, left me, and my heart began to beat with a nervous flutter. We were to be searched and smoked!

This was at present an unknown horror. A few moments later it became a real one. After a minute or so, a little light came into my place of imprisonment. The hatches had evidently been opened. I heard voices, and the searching began.

It was impossible for the Confederate soldiers to move about the cargo, that was packed so tightly; but by means of long poles, which they forced through the crevices between the bales of cotton, they explored every part of the vessel pretty thoroughly, and had it not been for the protecting beam of the vessel behind which I had taken refuge, my body would have been such a mass of bruises and wounds that I should probably have cried out from very pain. As it was, I rather laughed at the efforts of my enemies to bring me from my place of concealment.

While the guard were doing this, the captain jeered at them. "Didn't I tell you there wasn't any refugees on board my vessel! Poke away, but don't keep me so I'll lose the tide and can't get out through the Yankee blockaders to-night."

"All right!" said the officer in command of the guard-boat. "We'll give your hold a good half-hour's smoke, and if that doesn't bring any one, we'll let you go down the river."

The hatches were put on again, and I could hear the men going up on deck. As the light was cut off by the closed hatchways, a vile, suffocating, unendurable odor of smoking rosin and tar came to my nostrils. This grew denser and denser, until every breath that I drew seemed to contain no oxygen but all smoke. The perspiration came from every pore of my body. A black soot settled upon me and filled my nostrils. I could feel my eyes grow large in their sockets. Racking pains shot through my head and back. I was too feeble to cry out, or I should have screamed for deliverance. Fainting, I sank down in my place of concealment. I was almost asphyxiated! Suddenly, as my head became lower, I felt a cold current of air fanning my cheek.

Greedily as a starving man seizes food did I inhale this. It was the breath of life, and issued from a small aperture in an iron rod that came down and fitted into a socket in the deck. Instead of being solid, this was, for greater lightness, in the form of a tube. A portion of this tube had been broken away, which left free communication with the upper air above. I glued my mouth to the aperture, and once more began to live. I could defy not only the searching, but the smoking of my enemies.

I lay there and sucked in the invigorating air from above, while around me, for the next fifteen minutes, was an atmosphere of soot and smoke in which no man could have lived. After a time the hatches were reopened. No cries having been heard, and no one having crawled out to surrender himself, the guard-boat departed. I made myself as comfortable as circumstances would permit, and about two hours afterward the boat stopped again and anchored behind Fort Fisher. I knew that it must become dark night, and that consequently several hours must elapse, before the boat would venture to leave the protection of the Confederate guns.

To my astonishment it seemed to me hardly an hour before the vessel's engines were again in motion. She was moving through the water once more.

What was the meaning of this—it could not be possible the captain would dare to run his vessel through the blockading squadron in open daylight? She must, for some unknown reason, be returning to Wilmington !

As this horrid thought ran through me, I gave a gasp of despair, but after a moment became calmer and determined to find out. Anything was better than suspense.

I began to crawl through, or rather over the cotton toward the hatchway. A little light coming from it, as it had not been carefully closed, guided my movements. After half an hour's desperate battle with the cotton bales, squeezing between them and the deck, I arrived at the hatchway. Looking up I became convinced it was really daylight. I consulted my watch. It showed the hour of 5 P.M.

What unforeseen thing had happened? That I must discover. Cautiously I forced the hatchway further off, and, standing on the cotton bales below, squeezed myself through upon the lower deck.

There was no one here to discover me. After making sure of that, I carefully ascended the ladder, and, peering out upon the upper deck, saw, as well as I was able for the surrounding bales of cotton, that there was something white and fleecy in the air about me. For a moment I thought the ship must be on fire and deserted by her crew. Next, my eyes being blinded by the light after the inky blackness of the vessel's hold, I imagined that it was flakes of cotton liberated from their bales in some unknown manner, floating about me. A few moments after I gave a gasp of astonishment and joy—my eyes had resumed their functions. I saw what was really taking place.

In a dense, heavy white ocean fog, the blockade-runner was boldly attempting to run unseen through the Federal squadron that barred her passage to the open sea.

Whether the blockade-runner escaped or was captured by the United States vessels, I was out of the Confederacy in any event!

I staggered upon the deck feeling once more a free man. The crew were all at their places. The captain near the pilot, who stood at the wheel, bringing two small lights that were placed upon the beach half a mile away into a line, or what is nautically termed "into one."

When this was done, we were in the true channel leading to the ocean.

The second officer saw me, and silently supported me to where the captain was. That gentleman regarded me for a moment and whispered : "Give him something to drink. The poor devil's dying. He looks like a smoked herring. Haven't time to attend to him now !" and then gazed with the pilot anxiously out to sea.

My appearance justified the skipper's words. I was covered with black soot that made me look almost a negro. My mouth was parched with the heat of the lower hold ; my tongue hung out of it bronzed by thirst ; my body was fainting with weakness. I could only gasp, "Water !"

It was given me. I revived and became hungry. The cook took compassion on me, and gave me some hard tack and meat. I sat upon the deck, silently munching this and regaining my strength. As I ate, I watched the picture before me with intense eagerness. The vessel was making her way slowly from under the guns of Fort Fisher into the circle of Federal blockading vessels that were presumed to lie just out of the range of the Confederate artillery. I say presumed to lie, because the fog was so dense that not one of them could be seen. Through this fog the boat glided, her deck as silent as if she were manned by the dead, though every sailor of the crew was on the alert, and every motion showed intense excitement.

The pilot and captain were at the wheel, and the directions were given to the engineer in whisper through a speaking tube ; the sounding of the bell might indicate our whereabouts to some neighboring Federal cruiser.

Though it was only five o'clock in the afternoon, this fog was as good a protection, if not a better, than the darkness of night. As I stood leaning against a cotton bale, my nerves seemed to be more powerful than those of ordinary men, my excitement was so great. I caught a motion of the second officer of the vessel, who stood near me.

He went forward silently to the captain and touched his arm, and looking through the mist, I saw a light glimmering in the fog about a hundred yards away.

The captain muttered, as the second officer pointed this out to him: "The light of a Yankee flag-ship. She has to keep a light, as she is at anchor. Some of the cruisers might run into her."

We passed the light. Receiving no hail, and hearing no commotion on her decks, I gave a sigh of relief, which the captain echoed. But not a minute after this my heart gave a jump. There was a whizzing sound through the air ; for a moment I thought that it must be a shot, but looking into the heavens, I saw the fiery tail of a rocket fly through the mist.

"Curse her!" growled the captain; "she suspects something, and has sent up a signal. There will be a lot of them around here and around us in a few minutes!"

With that he whispered something down the speaking-tube to the engine-room. The vessel seemed suddenly to double her speed and fly through the white, thick clouds of vapor that were around her. But now, to the horror of every one on board, this vapor, as we sped along, seemed to grow lighter and lighter, and the captain muttered to himself : " My God ! the fog is rising ! "

Then the pilot grew pale, and whispered : " There is a very good chance of our being captured this trip."

The captain muttered, " I have made three in-and-out runs this year, and d——d if I will be captured this trip, or any other ! "

As for me, my heart was as light as the dancing waves through which we rode. If captured, I would be sent north; and if we reached Nassau, I could take a vessel for New York. I was out of the Confederacy, that was certain !

My joy was so great that it was impossible to keep it out of my face, and the second officer as he passed gave me a scowl, and said : " What are you looking so d——d happy for ? "

As for the captain, he seemed to be thinking deeply, and turning some plan for escape over in his brain.

The vessel continued her speed. Suddenly a low, dusky outline appeared in the mist upon the port side of us. Both the captain and pilot gave a start, and grasped the handles of the wheel more firmly. The next instant a cry of the second officer and a wave of his hand caused me to look to starboard. Another low, dark outline could be seen upon that side of us. Both, however, were a little forward of us—one upon our port, and the other upon our starboard bow. " Two cursed Yankee cruisers ! " muttered the second officer.

The next instant thunder apparently broke into the mist. The lightning flashed, and the thunderbolts seemed to fly through the air.

The English captain gave a low chuckle, and said : " D——n them, those two Yankee beggars are peppering each other ! " (for not a shot came near us). " Now they will be so occupied they won't notice me."

He whispered something to the engine-room, turned a few spokes of the wheel, and the little blockade-runner seemed to revolve upon her axis and return over the path by which she had come.

"What are you doing ? " gasped I.

" Going back to Fort Fisher as quick as we can," muttered the second officer. " We will try it again to-night ! "

These words almost made my heart stop still. Going

back to Fort Fisher! Going back to the Confederacy, from which I had escaped! Would I be able to conceal myself, and sail out again on their next attempt? The chances were not one in ten thousand, with my escape known in Wilmington, and Mr. Peter Bassett upon my trail.

My only hope now was that *we should be captured!*

In returning, we were compelled to run close to the Federal flag-ship again, and the mist was not quite so heavy.

With the courage born of desperation, as we neared the admiral's flag-ship I shrieked out wildly to the top of my lungs: "Ship ahoy! Stop this blockade-runner!"

My voice rang out through the still air, causing a commotion on the Federal flag-ship that I could see as well as hear, but causing more commotion and more surprise upon the decks of the blockade-runner.

A pattering hail of musket balls began to fall upon us. The United States marines had opened fire!

"Ship ahoy!" I cried again.

I could see the red-faced English captain dancing a jig of rage as he stood at the wheel. The second officer was cursing, and running toward me, a belaying pin in his hand.

I cried: "Ship ahoy! Stop this block——"

At this instant a flash of lightning seemed to strike my brain. I reeled and fell upon the deck. My last fleeting, conscious glance saw the second officer with his belaying pin raised for another blow.

Then the mist seemed to close around me and night to come upon me. There was a surging in my ears, a roaring of waves in my brain, and——nothing!

CHAPTER VIII.

THE SHOVEL OR THE RIFLE?

"CHUCK that corpse into a wagon!"

The voice seemed familiar, but I was so sick, so dizzy, and such burning pains shot through my head, that I was unable to speak.

" Pitch that corpse into a wagon, I say, quick ! "

The voice seemed very familiar to me. I felt myself thrown into something in a very unceremonious manner, and gave a groan.

" Hello ! By Jove he's a tough one ! " was the next remark, and in the tones I recognized the voice of Peter Bassett. " Smoked, and poled, and knocked over the head with a belaying pin by a British skipper until he is nearly a mummy, and *still* alive ! I have half a mind to let him die, for the mean trick he played on me, but I reckon I had better fulfill my orders and get him back into a breathing condition if possible."

With that I felt my jaws forced open, and something trickled down my throat that seemed liquid fire, but apparently gave renewed life and vigor to my limbs, though my head still ached as though it would burst.

" What are you doing to me ? " I gasped.

" Giving you brandy, firstly, and carrying you back to the provost marshal at Wilmington, secondly. You are the slipperiest customer I ever tackled."

" Where am I ? " I muttered, dreamily.

" Just being toted on the ambulance through the streets of Wilmington, North Carolina. The British skipper was so cursed mad at your hallooing to the Yanks that he had not more than cast anchor before his boat brought you ashore and turned you over. He swears that after his hospitality to you, you are the most ungrateful cuss that ever trod his deck. If, from your desperation, he had not supposed we would shoot you as soon as we got hold of you, I reckon he would have tossed you overboard to the sharks."

All this came to me in a dreamy way. The throbbing in my brain was so severe that I did not care very much at that moment what was happening to me.

A few minutes after I found myself in the temporary Confederate prison at Wilmington. A surgeon attended me and said that in a week I would be fit to travel. I did not pay much attention to all this, but being carefully attended, and the young doctor being a man of skill, I in a few days became convalescent enough to think, and with thought came almost despair.

During my attempted escape from the Confederacy, I had been too excited to give much thought to anything but my movements. I had had no time for reflection. Now I began to think of the sweetheart I had lost, and loved, and for whom I had sacrificed so much. I knew I could expect little mercy from the Confederate Government —that my chances of getting north were now practically nothing ; that I would be either forced into the Confederate service to fight against the cause I regarded as right, or drag out the length of the war in some Confederate military prison. All that, however, seemed but little to me, now that I had once more got my thoughts upon Laura Peyton. I fell to dreaming about her in a desperate, sullen sort of manner. I believe I should have died of despair had I not heard the surgeon say, one day, that as soon as I was well enough for him to certify my ability to travel, I was to be sent to Charleston.

To Charleston ! I was going nearer to the girl from whom I had fled, but whose image had never left my mind, even in the excitement of the extraordinary adventures, uncertainties, and trials through which I had passed.

I asked the surgeon if he could tell me from where the orders had come for my removal.

" I believe they were brought here by the detective who caused your arrest."

This of course meant my friend Mr. Bassett. If I could but discover under whose instructions he was acting, or by what influence he had been detailed to prevent my escape from the Confederacy, I might be able to form an idea of my future fate.

Two days afterward I left Wilmington upon the train in the custody of the detective, and, weak as I was, proceeded to pump him as to the influence that had brought me to the condition I was now in. I had not been robbed of my money when arrested. Bassett, for a detective, was honest ; consequently, by means of my Federal greenbacks, that were as potent in the Confederacy as they were north of Mason and Dixon's line, I soon had Mr. Bassett in a sufficiently communicative mood for him to tell me he reckoned I had some powerful enemy among the high government officials.

" Do you mean Confederate army officials ? " I asked.

" Oh, no ; they are too busy fighting ; but it is somebody who has a big pull in Richmond."

" You don't know his name ? " I inquired.

"No ; and if I did I would not tell you ; but he is a big 'un, you can reckon on that."

The only enemy I had of such influence was Mr. Amos Pierson. The poorer the Confederacy grew, the richer he had become, and the army contractor had now even greater power than at the beginning of the war.

Amos Pierson had had me arrested ! Amos Pierson had prevented my escape north ! And fool that he was, Amos Pierson was bringing me nearer and nearer with each revolution of the car wheels to the girl I loved ! I felt happy in the thought that in my forlorn condition my luck was turning ; that after all it was fated I should not leave South Carolina until I had made her my bride.

When youth and hope pull the same way, the result is almost a certainty. In the two days that Mr. Bassett and I took to reach Charleston, health had again come to me. My spirits, before broken down, were elastic and buoyant. My body, that had been debilitated and enervated by disappointment and confinement, was rapidly regaining the elasticity and strength that should be in a man of twenty-eight who has not destroyed his vitality by disease, dissipation, nor luxury. I was strong enough to fight the battle of life and love once more as we ran into Charleston.

We arrived at this place about April 17th, nearly two weeks after the decisive repulse of the Federal monitors in their attack upon and bombardment of Fort Sumter and the neighboring batteries.

The town, as I looked at it in the bright, soft spring air of that April morning, would have seemed to me the Charleston I had known before the war, had it not been for its hurrying troops, the new batteries in connection with Moultrie to the left, the long lines of earthworks to the right, on the shores of Morris and James islands, ending in Battery Wagner ; between these Fort Sumter, sitting upon its granite rocks in the middle of the passage, the key to the defense of Charleston. I had not much time for reflection, for I was immediately placed in charge of the provost guard by Mr. Bassett, and hurried through the streets to the Charleston jail in the southeastern portion of the city.

A few Federal prisoners of war were in the jail yard at the time, though it was by no means crowded ; as it was

some months afterward, when a number of Union cap-
tives, officers and men, were brought in from Anderson-
ville and other prisons, in a vain attempt to prevent the
United States batteries on Morris Island from bombard-
ing the town.

To my astonishment I was placed in the fourth story
of the jail building—a portion that was entirely devoted
to the incarceration of deserters from the Confederate
army. I protested against this, telling the officer in
charge that I was no deserter, and asking to be confined
with the civil prisoners on the ground floor.

This, however, was immediately denied me. I had to
make myself as comfortable as possible where I was
placed. This I did by means of some of the greenbacks
I still had with me.

I asked the officer in command of the guard if I could
be permitted to communicate with Colonel Bee, of the
Adjutant General's department. After some hesitation,
he refused to carry or send any note, but informed me
that he would notify Colonel Bee that I was in the prison,
and in case that officer wanted to see me, he presumed I
would know it. That was all that I wished. Bee was
the last man to turn his back upon a friend when in distress or trouble.

Agreeable to my expectations, about an hour after this
Stuart Bee passed the guard and came up to see me. He
was looking very well, with the exception of a slight pale-
ness, caused by loss of blood, and carried his left arm in
a sling.

Noticing my look of anxiety, he gave a slight laugh and
said : " Bryant, a little present from your friends, the
Yanks. I got it at Fort Sumter about two weeks ago.
If it had not been for that, you would hardly have seen
me so soon ; but I am at present, fortunately for you, off
active duty on account of this. However, I will be
shortly in condition to return this compliment." And he
touched his bandaged arm.

I expressed my concern at his wound.

" Pooh ! pooh ! It is nothing ! Your case is a great
deal worse. Now," he said, taking me aside, " unless
you do something for yourself, I can do very little for
you, Bryant, old fellow. You did not take my advice,
and report for service as ordered, but attempted to

escape. At all events, that is what Bassett reports of your movements. Now that you are here, unless you do as I advise you, the chances are you will have, during this summer, a pretty warm time of it."

"What do you advise me to do?" I asked.

"Do what you are commanded. You will join the Confederate service. I believe I have influence enough to get you a staff appointment, as I promised you. Your engineering ability is well known, and can be made use of here in building fortifications. You will probably have no active fighting to do against *our enemies* the Yanks."

"And if I refuse to fight 'our enemies' the Yanks?" said I.

"Then all I can do is to make your lot as a prisoner as comfortable as possible. We are suffering, ourselves, for want of provisions and many comforts of life; you, as a prisoner, will scarcely receive as much, and will be, comparatively, badly off. Think of this matter. I will contrive to postpone your examination until to-morrow. Do as I ask you. It is the easiest way out of the scrape, old fellow. Meantime I will try to make your quarters more comfortable."

With this he left me. Half an hour afterward I had evidence of Bee's not having forgotten his promise.

I was removed to the second floor of the building where the Confederate officers and soldiers accused of military offenses were imprisoned. There I had a small room by myself, which had clean linen upon its bed. Soon after a good meal of corn bread, fresh beef, and coffee made from parched corn, showed me that as far as it was possible in a country that was slowly but surely losing all the comforts of life, my welfare had been taken care of by the generous Georgian.

The next morning Bee called again, and added to his arguments of the day before the following one, which caused me much mental anguish, though it did not shake the resolution I had made and kept for three years.

"I have been inquiring about your affair, Bryant," he said, "and it is rumored that the reason you remained south, was because of your engagement to Judge Peyton's daughter. You stayed here to win her, but her southern sentiments prevented your success, even though she loved you. From all I can find out, I am inclined to think she loves you still. If you join us, old boy, she'll adore you, and we will soon have a wedding. I'll be your best man—for even in these unhappy days we soldiers steal some time from Mars to devote to Cupid. You might just as well be happy and free as an officer of the Confederate army, and gain the woman you love, as to be a prisoner until the close of the war and lose her. Your examination will take place in about half an hour. Don't make a fool of yourself! Let love aid common sense!"

The time left me for reflection did not change my resolution. I had made up my mind how I must act. Duty and honor said one thing. Love might cry out the other as loud as it liked; my resolve was unchanged.

My interview with the Confederate provost marshal was very short, but by no means sweet. That officer said: "Mr. Bryant, I know everything in regard to your matter. We have a high respect for your ability as an engineer. You can be very useful to us. You were ordered to report at Charleston on the 10th of April. Seven days afterward you were brought here, having attempted to leave the Confederate lines without a passport, and under circumstances that indicated you intended to go north. Your resignation to the railroad company shows that you expected to leave the South."

Here he handed me the document that had been delivered by Caucus, as I instructed him, to the officials of the South Carolina Railway. "What have you to say to it?"

"Nothing!" replied I, "you are entirely correct in your surmise. I did intend to leave the Confederacy, because I do not wish to take service in any capacity against the government of the United States."

"Very well," continued he, "you are a deserter from our service. If you accept an appointment under the Confederacy, and take the oath of allegiance to our government, you will be put upon active duty in the army. Do you accept the same?"

"No!" I answered. "I will not enlist in the Confederate army."

"Very well. I shall report the case as it stands to the general in command." And with that he dismissed me under care of the guard again to my prison.

A week after this I was summoned before him once more.

"We have received orders from Richmond with regard to you," he said, "and I am sorry, Mr. Bryant, that they are of a kind that will be as unpleasant for me to carry out as they will be for you to endure. You refuse to enter the Confederate army, once more?"

"Yes!" I replied, "as firmly as I did two days ago, but I am very much obliged to you, colonel. I see you wish to give me a chance to escape some unpleasant position."

"You are entirely right, Mr. Bryant," he said, "but since you will not accept it, my orders are to imprison you here and place you, as a criminal laborer, under military guard upon the fortifications of this place."

"A criminal?" gasped I.

"Yes, such are my orders. 'Deserters are criminals.' Since the planters refuse to let us have all the negroes needed to complete the necessary fortifications, we want shovels as well as rifles to defend Charleston. You refuse to carry the rifle. You *shall* carry the shovel. *Good-by.*"

CHAPTER IX.

THE NIGHT ATTACK.

I HAD hardly reached the prison again, when Bee came to see me, and said: "You are very foolish in this matter, Bryant. Change your mind, and even at this moment I will try to make your fate a better one. There is some strong influence working against you, otherwise you would probably have been merely imprisoned here; but unless you consent to the terms offered you, there is no doubt that in a day or two you will be working on some of those sand batteries down the bay along with a gang of negroes. They talk of the yellow fever coming here this summer. You will lead the life of a slave. Unaccustomed as you are to hardship, I hardly think, old boy, that you will ever see your sweetheart again For God's sake, take my advice; I mean it for your good."

"No," I replied, for I had grown dogged in this matter. "Under no circumstances will I take the oath of allegiance to the Confederate Government!"

"Very well," he said; "you have made your bed, and it is a hard one." He wrung my hand and left me.

That evening I discovered, by the change in my treatment, what was to be my fate. I was again removed to the fourth floor of the building, which, even at this season of the year, was growing very hot and unpleasant.

Despite my expostulations, my clothes were removed, my money taken from me, and I was clad in the stripes of a convict. My rations were cut down to simple corn-meal, and I began to experience the bitterness and hopelessness of my fate.

The next morning I was hurried off with two or three more Confederate prisoners,—the very scum of the prison, who had been sentenced for dastardly crimes against social law—not the military offenses of soldiers,—and sent to join a gang of negroes who were working upon the fortifications being hastily erected on the sandy island named Morris, defended and dominated at that time by the Confederate Battery Wagner.

As we were marched ignominiously down to the tugboat, some of the more desperate of us being ironed, the contemptuous glances of the people in the streets of Charleston showed me that I now was regarded as a criminal. The treatment of the guard as they hustled us onto the little tug-boat indicated that they regarded me as one of the class among whom I was placed ; not a soldier, not even a civilian, but simply a convict. I was very glad when, a few moments after, the tug left her dock and took me away from the people who, attracted by curiosity, gazed at us. It is very difficult to feel like a hero in the dress of a felon. I was becoming ashamed.

We ran down the harbor, passing the old-fashioned, ineffective Castle Pinckney to the left, then Battery Ripley, and, gliding along the south shore near Fort Johnston, passed between Battery Greig and the grim walls of Fort Sumter, which still frowned defiance, though somewhat shattered by the bombardment of Union monitors. A few minutes after, rounding Cummings' Point, we ran down the shore of Morris Island, and landed at Fort Wagner.

Here the Confederates needed not only rifles but shovels. We were to work the shovels.

This island is about three miles in length, and runs from Battery Greig on the north to a creek or estuary on the south which separates it from Folly Island.

This inlet is of sufficient size and depth to be impassable to an attacking party, unless in boats and protected by armed vessels. Morris Island has a varying width of from several hundred yards to perhaps a mile, but toward the west runs into a mass of creeks and marshes impracticable for the movement of troops. The ocean side of the island is composed of numbers of sandhills or dunes of varying size, some of them forty or fifty feet in height, perhaps more. These are all white, glistening, flinty, burning sand, except where covered by scrubby trees. The topography of Folly Island, at that time occupied by the Federal forces, is of the same general character.

On landing, we were marched, or rather driven, to the southern end of the island, where we were placed at work upon some light batteries that were being prepared hurriedly for Confederate guns. Here, under a brilliant southern sun the glistening sand became during the day hot as the surface of a winter stove. The nights, fortunately, in this later part of April, were cooler, and gave us some relief.

But as summer came on, even these grew hot. From the time we landed, our lives became a fearful drudgery which was never suffered to relax ; during the day, filling sand bags and throwing up embankments; by night, fighting sand fleas for rest, slumber and forgetfulness. Our rations—corn meal and rancid bacon—were such that had I not been absolutely driven to it by starvation, I could not have eaten a mouthful. As day after day passed, all this became a frightful, driving monotony. The Confederate officers, forced to haste in the erection of their batteries by the evident preparations that were being made on Folly Island to attack them, drove us harder and harder in our labor. These men did not spare their own muscles and their own blood; then why should they spare us convicts and slaves ?

The summer advanced. The nights and days became hotter and hotter, the labor more cruel and unremitting, our rations smaller and more nauseating. Morris Island was now a purgatory. Then came the Federal attack, and this purgatory became a hell. We were shot at from the Union batteries upon Folly Island. The little blood left in our poor, half-naked bodies by the swarms of voracious mosquitoes was drained from some of us by bursting Federal shells. When first upon the island, in the day there was only time for labor, but at night I used to think of the woman I loved. Afterward, the dull monotony of passive misery seemed to take possession of me. I thought of nothing but of keeping alive till I escaped. I began to look longingly at the United States flag floating scarcely a mile from me, but what a mile ! —a few hundred yards of white sand, a deep inlet a quarter of a mile wide, and more uncovered sand to that Federal flag. A thousand to one I would be shot before I reached even the inlet. Notwithstanding the desperate nature of the enterprise, I believe I should have attempted it at night, had not about this time the increased rapidity with which we were worked driven all else but the desire for rest from my mind when permitted respite from a toil that now became utterly exhaustive.

The activity on Folly Island indicated that the Confederates were right in hurrying their preparations for defense. One night—I cannot be exactly sure as to the exact time, because I had failed in my misery to count the days or take record of the months—one burning-hot night we heard the sound of the chopping of a thousand axes upon Folly Island. In spite of the shelling of the Confederate batteries, this sound continued all night, and the next morning it seemed as though a magician's wand had waved. The woods in our front across the inlet were all cut down, uncovering to us a long line of Federal batteries, crowned with artillery and heavily manned. Between these and the Confederates an immediate cannonade began, which continued at intervals for nearly a week.

At the end of this time four low, black-looking vessels, each one bearing upon its deck a single black turret, appeared off the bar. I had never before seen any ships like them, but I knew they were monitors. The fortifications were now as nearly complete as they could be made under the heavy fire of the Federal troops, and we of the shovel were all marched up the island to give place to those who used the musket, in the form of gray Confederate infantry.

As we entered the bombproofs of Fort Wagner, I could see the monitors steaming in over the bar and taking up a position north of the southern portion of Morris Island. The next moment a tremendous bombardment began. Long lines of barges, towed by steam launches or propelled by oars, shot out from Folly Island, carrying some thousands of troops. Despite the Confederate fire, which cut lanes in their blue ranks, these were landed and formed upon the sandy beach.

This cannonade continued while we were driven along the island to Fort Greig, then onto boats, and ferried over like cattle to grim old Sumter, to work on its fortifications, now beginning to disintegrate under the Union guns.

As we entered the fort, I gazed at Morris Island. The flag of the United States was flying at its southern end, over the batteries upon which I had been working the day before.

The Federal forces had now to accomplish the most difficult portion of their work : that was the capture of Fort Wagner. Their iron-clads steamed in, and for thirty days and nights rained the largest projectiles in use at that time upon both Sumter and this sand battery that barred their passage to Charleston.

During this time, in Sumter, the same grinding toil fell upon us. We labored like cattle, dismounting and removing guns, filling up rents and fissures in the fort's granite walls with their very débris knocked about us by Federal cannon—all this under a fire that was simply infernal. Like the galley slaves of old, we toiled and died without the reward of soldiers' gallantry or the honor of soldiers' deaths. We had ten times the discomforts and twice the danger of the troops in the garrison. If there was a scarcity of provisions, whose rations were cut down? The convicts'. Were the bombproofs full, for whom was there no shelter from Federal shot and shell? The negroes and criminals. By this time, misery had made me scarcely human.

This continued for some thirty or forty days, when one morning I saw the Confederate flag was not flying upon Wagner, that lay in full view from Sumter, across the channel. Half an hour afterward the stripes and stars were hoisted upon it, and I knew the southerners had evacuated Morris Island.

All this I looked upon with listless interest, until I chanced to hear a conversation between two Confederate officers. One said : "Since the Yankee army has got Wagner, I reckon the Yankee fleet will try to get us."

"Then," replied the other, "if they are fools enough for that, we'll get them ! How do you imagine they'll try it ?"

"Boats, of course ! " muttered the other ; and then he cried : "Look out ! That was a nasty one !" as a shell from one of the monitors knocked over a ton of granite from the crumbling wall upon a working party on the fort. Under this lump of stone, as they walked away, I could see two or three writhing bodies.

These words had set my brain going again. If the Federal boats made an attack, even if driven off, I might climb out of one of the casemates, and perhaps escape with them—if they captured Sumter, I was free any way.

I began to look round me and see what the chances of success were. The preparations made for the defense against such an attempt made me know it could not succeed. The fort had been battered into crumbling ruins. No heavy guns upon its battlements were in condition to be fired ; but in these ruins were bombproofs impregnable to either bombardment or assault. The crumbling walls could still support light field-pieces. These loaded with grape and canister, were so placed as to sweep with a cross-fire the various faces of the fort. Hand-grenades were piled about in convenient places. The few companies of artillery that had garrisoned the fort during its bombardment had been replaced by some of Colquitt's Georgia infantry. Muskets, not cannons, were to be the weapons now used in Fort Sumter.

I continued my observations, and as the officers appeared to regard me more as a machine than a man, discovered from their conversation that upon a signal the batteries of Johnston, Moultrie, and Sullivan's Island had all been trained to sweep the faces of Fort Sumter, the direction and elevation of their guns marked and noted so that they could fire with the same accuracy of range at night as by day.

In this fire no boat attack could succeed. I therefore made my arrangements to join the Federal launches in their inevitable retreat.

For this purpose I selected a broken-down embrasure, the rubbish from which ran in a gradual slope to the water. It was easy of ascent as well as descent, and would be sure to tempt some of the officers of the attacking party to try a landing. I noted that no gun could easily be trained upon it. Through this embrasure I would join the Union boats. This being settled I fell to waiting for the night that I hoped would give me liberty.

Notwithstanding the desperate fatigue and labor of the day, I lay awake, all the night after I had heard this conversation, looking for the Union boats ; but nothing came save an occasional shot from their monitors.

The next day I could see something was expected to take place. The hurried manner in which we were worked, filling hand-grenades and placing bags of sand about many of the embrasures of the fort, in order to prevent musket-balls or grape-shot from the Federal launches entering them, all told this.

As the evening drew on, the night became dark. Then the hail from boats coming down Charleston harbor was heard, and a reinforcement of some hundred more of Colquitt's Georgians came into the fort accompanied by several officers who had volunteered for this night's particular service. Among them, I thought I heard the voice of my friend Bee, but was unable to communicate with him, as immediately after this we convicts, together with such negroes as were in the fort, were marched under guard to a distant portion of the works.

All this told me that by some means General Beauregard, who commanded the fortifications of Charleston, was aware that this night had been selected for the boat attack.

Sneaking past the guard, who were now intent only upon noises coming from the sea, I crawled to the embrasure I had selected, and looked out over the surface of the water. Nothing was to be seen save a few sparks of fire ascending lazily into the air some miles out to sea from the smoke-stack of one of the Federal vessels, and the low, black hull of a Confederate iron-clad that moved slowly past me to take a position some half mile away, where her guns could cover one of the angles of the fortification. Despite my fatigue, the excitement kept my eyes from closing. I waited and watched for all of three hours, but about this time, overcome by lack of sleep my eyes closed, and I fell into an uneasy slumber.

From this a noise that seemed to shatter my ears awakened me. The light guns of the fort had been discharged, and a rolling fire of musketry was pelting bullets through the darkness into the water for a hundred yards or more from the base of the fort. Suddenly a single rocket went into the air. The next instant the faces and angles of the fort were swept by every projectile known to modern warfare. The Confederate guns on Sullivan's Island had opened on us, followed immediately by Ripley, Johnston and the Confederate iron-clads. Under our bombproofs the garrison was safe. Heaven defend the Union boats outside !

The water for several hundred yards about became a mass of foam under the bursting shells and solid shot that plowed it up. Then, by the light of an exploding bomb, for the first time I discovered the Federal boats dashing toward us in several divisions. As they entered the fire, some of the barges sank, the screams of their drowning crews arising over the babel of sound. Pelted by musketry, plowed up by cannon shot, detachments of these boats with a cheer pulled for the attack.

One division headed by a young officer came straight for the embrasure from which I was looking, favoring the sand-bags that protected me with a volley.

As they approached, hand-grenades were thrown upon them from the fort.

The Federal officer cried : " That casemate is our best chance. Give way, men ! " They forced their boats up on the scarp and débris at the foot of my embrasure. As they leaped on shore a solid shot from Moultrie crashed through one barge and a bursting hand-grenade tore up the bottom of another. I sprang out to join them, and, as I did so, a bullet from the officer's revolver grazed my hand. The next instant the boats that were following him were either destroyed or else retreated out to sea.

A dropping musketry fire from the battlements above

struck down several of the sailors and marines about him.
The launches that were following retreated into the darkness. The young officer looked at his sinking boats, and
saw that there was no chance for success. I was about
to beg him to retreat, and to tell him I would join him,
when to my horror and astonishment, he handed me his
sword and cried: "Tell your men to cease firing! I
am here unsupported. To save my men, I surrender to
you."

Stunned by disappointment, I looked at the white
handkerchief one of the sailors was waving, and saw the
boats in which the Federals had come sink into deep
water by the scarp of the fort. The order to cease firing
was given above; a detachment of Confederate infantry
appeared at the embrasure, headed by my friend Bee.

He cried out: "The only way to save our prisoners'
lives is to take them into the fort!" For the shot from
Moultrie and the Confederate batteries around the harbor still hailed upon the outside of Sumter. I came up
first. As the Federal lieutenant was dragged into the
embrasure with his men, he said to Bee: "I cannot give
you my sword, as I have already surrendered it to one of
your men, a very gallant fellow who attacked us single-handed; but if I had had support from the rest of the
boats—curse 'em!—I'd have fought my way into that
embrasure!"

The next instant Bee in the darkness dragged me
along to the commanding officer to receive a reward for
my gallantry.

Almost the first thing I recollect after this was standing in a circle of Confederates, and hearing Bee say:
"This is the man who, single-handed, attacked the Federal boat's crew!"

Then an astonished laugh came to my ears, the commanding officer saying: "By the Lord! it's a convict
that has done all this! Gallantry's contagious. Some of
our slaves will soon be capturing a Yankee regiment!"

Though Bee took a good look at me upon this speech,
still he did not recognize me.

I said: "Colonel Bee, I am a convict, but, you know,
not a criminal, though compelled to labor here as one;"
Then I turned and walked sullenly away, and joined the
gang of slaves and convicts; for the cruel disappoint-

ment of the night had almost maddened me. I hated every one who wore the Confederate uniform.

Half an hour afterward one of the guards touched me on the shoulder, and said : "Colonel Bee wishes to speak to you."

I followed him, and found the gallant Georgian about to reëmbark in one of the boats that were taking back a portion of the troops to Charleston.

He tcok me aside, and said : "Did you really attack the Federal sailors ? Do you now intend to join us ? If so, I can report this to the commanding officer, and, I think, under the circumstances, have your sentence revoked."

"Does this imply my taking the oath of allegiance, and joining the Confederate army ? "

"Certainly."

"Then I must refuse."

"You had better reconsider. Your lot here is a hard one, for, Heaven knows ! I would hardly recognize you —you are so terribly changed ! "

"You need not take any trouble on my account," I said. "I do not intend to join you. I did not attack the United States sailors. I went to join *them*, and to attack *you*, but to my disappointment, they surrendered to me."

"Very well," said Bee, curtly, after a little laugh. "If you won't help yourself, I can do nothing more for you ! "

He turned and walked to the boat, never looking back.

I could see that my sullen manner had irritated the man who had tried to be my friend as far as circumstances permitted him.

Then the guard took me again to the wretched hole in which we convicts and slaves were herded. I lay down, broken in mind, broken in body, broken in heart. The chance I had longed for, and planned for, had failed me. I was still a prisoner, doomed to slave in a Confederate fort.

BOOK III.

How I Won Her.

CHAPTER X.

SHE CAME!

THE next day the gang of laborers with which I worked was moved out of the fort. At dusk, to avoid the Federal fire, we were embarked on boats towed by a steam tug up Charleston Harbor, and I thought we were going to the town ; but, instead, our voyage was continued to a little creek called "Wappoo," that empties into the Ashley River, opposite the city.

Moving up this as far as boats could go, we were landed and marched a mile or two that night, to some sheds evidently prepared for us, given our miserable rations of poor corn meal and poorer bacon, and lay down in some straw, like dogs in a kennel, to sleep.

Early the next morning, under guard, we were set to work on some fortifications about a mile from Fort Pemberton, on Stono River. These were being hurriedly completed. Having failed in the reduction of Fort Sumter, the Union forces might now make some attempt to come to Charleston, *via* Stono River. It was much pleasanter here than on the sand dunes of Morris Island. There was running water, green trees, and an absence of that deafening sound that came upon us day and night from the Federal guns. Bad as it was, the place was a great improvement upon where we had previously worked. These fortifications were not heavy earthworks, like those at Wagner, or on Morris Island, but were long lines of intrenchments fitted to protect an infantry force in the open field, though, at convenient places, batteries were erected in which guns could be placed as needed to resist any Federal advance.

Curiously enough, my health under these circumstances became better. The greenness of the trees pleased me after the white sand dunes of Morris Island. The running water sounded sweetly to me, and I became stronger and better each day. I had grown accustomed to hardship and hard fare. Besides, my life was given a certain variety by the number of people I saw passing along the country roads, this place being entirely out of the range of Federal guns. Ladies, even, sometimes passed that way, though I took but little notice of them, and my life was monotonous toil.

I was awakened from this monotony by a sudden shock. One day, laboring on an earthwork that ran close to and commanded a long, yellow, dusty road, I heard the sound of hoofs upon it. Chancing to look up, my gaze became petrified and fixed upon four figures on horseback, made indistinct by a surrounding cloud of dust. One was a red-headed negro ; another looked like that of Bee the Georgian. Then cantered behind a youth with an empty sleeve, and last—*her form !* For a second I thought myself going mad, that it was an hallucination.

But her face became more and more distinct, the lovely eyes grew familiar to me, and *her* voice came to me. " Arthur, are you sure this is the right way ? "

At these words existence seemed at first a dream, then floated away. The shovel fell from my hand—the earth seemed to strike me.

The next thing I remember was the guard saying :

" Why, the poor devil must have got a sunstroke ! He fell down just as you come up, miss ! "

Then Laura Peyton's voice cried : " Quick ! Place him by this spring. The water will revive him ! "

I opened my eyes, and found myself in a small grove, through which a pretty little stream flowed down to the swamp that bordered Wappoo Creek, near the place where I had been working. The cold water revived me. I lay upon the grass. She was gazing at me and muttering " Poor fellow ! " but there was no recognition in her eyes. Caucus was bathing my face with water.

As he did so, the negro began to tremble and turn

dusky. Though he said nothing aloud, his lips muttered: "Fo' de Lord!"

A moment after the guard said: "Git up and back to work. I can't wait for you any longer. Git up!"

I did not move. I would have died before I left her without her knowing me.

"Git up!" and the fellow would have kicked me had she not stepped between us.

"This poor creature is sick, worn out—can't you see it! Are your eyes not human?" she said, standing over me in the plain homespun dress these days of pro· longed war had brought to all the ladies of the South.

"The officers are inspecting of us. I'm responsible for him ; he must come with me. Git up, you sneaking skunk!" muttered the man. "Git up!" and he raised his hand.

"Don't you dare touch him!" she cried. "My brother, Captain Peyton, is one of the officers inspecting you, Colonel Bee the other. I'll be responsible for this man's custody. Can't you see he's too weak to move ? Go back to your duty!"

"All right, miss, if you say so!" muttered the man. Remember, you'll see he comes back. Don't git me into the guard-house!"

"I'll see you are safe."

"Very well, miss," and the man returned to the in· trenchments.

He had no sooner disappeared in the trees than Cau· cus, whose eyes had been rolling wildly, suddenly cried : "Fo' de Lord! Massa Bryant!" and fell to kissing my hand, while she who had been gazing at me with a look all of pity and naught of recognition, suddenly grew pale and gasped: "My heaven!" then commenced to sob and wring her hands, and would have flown to me.

But I waved her off, and said : "Keep away—don't touch me. The filth of the prison is on me!"

And she muttered, "I don't care!" and would have soothed me with pitying tears, but as she came toward me she stopped and shuddered, looked at my striped dress, hes· itated, turned pale and gasped : "Why, *you are a convict!*"

"Yes, a convict for loving my country—for loving you! This striped dress is a present from your admirer —Amos Pierson's influence has brought me to this!"

6

" Amos Pierson ! " she cried. " He has again tried to obtain my consent to marry him. It was reported you were dead, as you had gone out to sea in a blockade-runner, which was destroyed by Federal vessels."

" Yes, Amos Pierson ! " said I. between my teeth, " Amos Pierson ! But, thank God ! his influence has brought me back to South Carolina—to you ! Laura, you refused him,—was it for me ? Was it for my sake ? Do you still, in spite of all," muttered I, for the girl was panting and sobbing in a way that gave me hope, " do you still——" I looked around. Caucus had disappeared. " Do you still, in spite of the North and the South, do you still love me ? "

She said nothing. I was trembling with disappointment, when in a flash she turned toward me and held up her finger. The sunlight through the treetops illumined it, and I saw upon it the engagement ring that she had dropped upon the greensward the day I parted from her in Columbia six months before.

Despite the rags and filth that covered me, I would have seized her in my arms, but at this moment the bushes that lined the stream were parted and Stuart Bee gazed upon us.

As he looked, a grin partly of astonishment, partly of good-nature, ran over his handsome countenance. He turned hurriedly back and I heard his voice saying : " Arthur, your sister is not here. We must look for her somewhere else ! "

As he did this, the sergeant of the guard forced his way through the brush, crying out to me : " You lazy sneak, you have been twenty minutes loafing here ! Back to work, at once ! "

A flash of rage was in my sweetheart's face. In another moment she would have confronted this man, her brother would have heard her, and there would have been a *dénouement* when Bee at this moment, looking over his shoulder, said sternly : " That man is worn out with work. Give him an hour's rest, or you will have to put him in the hospital, sergeant."

" Very well, sir," replied that functionary, touching his cap. " He has generally done his share, and I'll be easy on him this time ! "

He went back to his men. I could hear Bee and

Arthur walk off to their horses. Laura and I were alone together once more.

" Do you know that officer ? " she suddenly asked.

"Who, Stuart Bee ?" replied I. " He has been my only friend."

" He is still your friend—*our* friend," she cried. " He must have planned this meeting for us. He it was who obtained my brother's appointment to make the inspection of the fortifications here, and persuaded me to come with him."

" It was for my sake, Laura ! God bless him ! " I cried, as remorse seized me for the words I had uttered to him when last we met ; "but we will not be long uninterrupted. I must say all I have to very quickly."

I told her my adventures that had brought me to the state in which she saw me ; this very rapidly, and only interrupted by sighs of sympathy and exclamations of horror from Laura.

When it was over she said : " Lawrence, you must end this martyrdom at once ! "

" Yes, by perjuring myself, and becoming a Confederate soldier ! "

" No—not that way ! Though I am a southern girl—— not that way ! I should not respect you if you took that way now."

" Then how ? "

" I can't tell, yet. All I know is, that I could not exist thinking of you as I see you now. In some way I must save you,—in some way I *will* save you ! "

" You love me ? " I gasped.

" I'll talk of nothing now but how to save you ! "

" You love me ? " I begged.

" I hear my brother calling me ! I must go, or he will find us here ! "

" You love me ? " I cried.

" Yes, " she said. " I love you, and will save you ! "

I seized her hand in mine and pressed my parched, hot, burning lips upon it. As I did so, both a tear and a kiss fell on my face.

Arthur's voice was heard calling : " Laura, where are you ? " She turned from me and ran through the grove in the opposite direction to the road, apparently intending to come out at some distant point in answer to her brother's call.　Her tears had unloosed the fountains of my heart for the first time in all my misery.

Half an hour afterward I staggered out to the line of men, shoveling sand upon the Confederate earthworks. There was no sign of either her, her brother, or Caucus; still I shoveled away with a better heart than I had ever had before in the rebel trenches, for I had faith in the woman I loved fulfilling her promise and finding for me a way to freedom.

CHAPTER XI.

THE RED-HEADED NEGRO.

For two days I waited.　On the morning of the third, as we were being routed out to our work, I thought I heard a familiar negro voice.

The next moment the sergeant of the guard said: " Hello, here's a disobedient nigger!　To work in the trenches for punishment, eh?　You red-headed rascal, I'll take the spunk out of you!"

" Fo' de Lord! go easy on me, massa!"

No one took any interest in this matter, as it was a common habit of planters in the neighborhood to aid the Confederate cause by donating to it the labor of their insubordinate slaves; as for me, it filled me with hope. For the negro sent to work in the trenches was Caucus, and I guessed he had some communication for me. Unfortunately, however, he was told off to work on a different part of the fortifications, and I got no chance to communicate with him until night.　Our sleeping arrangements were very primitive.　We lay down in a long shed in any part that was convenient, the guard giving but little attention, except to see that we did not escape; consequently I soon worked myself alongside the red-headed negro.　He seemed at first in almost too much trouble to speak to me.

In answer to my inquiries, he only muttered: " Golly, if I knowed dis, I'd never no way come heah.　Dey worked de life out o' me to-day, an' dis grub ain't fit for a buzzard to chew!"

" You have something to tell me?"

"Yas ; but de sergeant said he'd tie me up by de thumbs—— "

"Speak—quick ! What message have you for me ?"

"Well, jes' let me get de aches out of my arms an' legs. Lord, how dey worked me ! It ain't possible you libed six months in dis kind of way, Massa Bryant ! "

" That is the reason I want to get out of it. Quick ! what communication have you for me ?"

" Well," he said, " don't I want to get out ob it quick too? De missus sent you dis," and he handed me a little packet.

Watching my opportunity I read the note. It was simply,

" Do as Caucus tells you."

Besides this, the packet contained the same identical roll of greenbacks I had sent my sweetheart and asked her to use on my leaving Columbia.

" Your mistress says," I whispered to him, " I am to do as you tell me.—What am I to do ?"

"Get out of heah, quick. I'se got a boat ready to take you down de Stono ribber to de Yanks."

" But how are we to get out of here ?"

" Well, dat's what you got to find out. If I'd a knowed what it was, I'd neber hab come myself, do' she'd begged me on her shins for an hour; but you must get out to-night."

Get out to-night ! The proposition was a sudden one.

Get out to-night without having a bullet put through my body ? As I looked at the line of Confederate sentries, with their loaded muskets, that prevented any escape of the negroes or convicts, the proposition seemed an absurd one.

I had never before thought of escaping from the guards, because, without friends and without money, it had always seemed to me an impossibility to reach the Union lines ; but now, as I reflected on the matter, my views suddenly changed.

The nights had been growing colder and colder, as we were now getting well into the month of November. Large camp fires each evening were built for the comfort of the guard. The wood for these had been brought every day by a detail under guard ; but to-day, for some reason, this had been omitted or forgotten. The stock of fuel was not sufficient for the night's use.

At the very moment I was planning escape, I heard the

sergeant directing some of his men to take a few of the laborers and get in a supply for the night. The soldiers, not wishing to take too much trouble, roused up and ordered out those of the prisoners nearest the door of the shed.

I whispered to Caucus to get up, come with me, and join the gang.

"I can't; I's too tired. Doan want no more work to-day. I's neber been used to de life ob a field hand."

"Come with me, if you want to get out of here to-night. The sergeant 'll tie you up by the thumbs to-mor-row," I whispered in his ear, supplementing my argu-ment with a vigorous kick, for I was thoroughly enraged at Caucus' indifference.

With a grunt, partly of rage and partly of pain, he got up and followed me.

We soon found ourselves in the wood squad guarded by three or four Confederate soldiers with loaded muskets, and marched off to some neighboring timber. I whispered to Caucus to keep close to me, whatever else he did.

Fortunately for us, the timber was quite thick about here, and we were ordered to spread through it and get the wood which had already been cut down and piled in various places. This we were to bring to a place indicated for our meeting just out in the open ground. We were divided into three gangs, a Confederate soldier with a loaded gun going with each one of these; the fourth, a corporal, remaining at the place to which we were told to bring the wood.

In the undergrowth at night it was a difficult matter for one man to keep his eye on three or four, and watch-ing my opportunity I gave Caucus a signal, then dropped down into the thick foliage, and crawled on my hands and knees followed by the negro.

I felt pretty sure that our absence would not be noticed until the gangs had brought the wood to the place of meeting. That would give us at least twenty minutes' start of any pursuit.

As I crawled along followed by Caucus, I asked him: "What route are we to take to your boat on the Stono River?"

His reply astonished me. He said: "Golly! I's too tired to go dar now. It's more'n a mile away."

"Look here," I said, "if they catch us, you will be shot as well as I."

"Golly! do you tink dey'll shoot *me?* "

"I know they will."

"Den dey's got to cotch me fust!" and from this time on the vigor of the negro astounded me.

He started off through the brushwood at a pace that made it difficult for me to keep up with him.

After about five minutes more of this travel, we entered the swamp that borders Wappoo Creek. We did this none too soon, for at this moment the firing of the guard indicated that our escape had been noticed.

Following Caucus by a path that he apparently knew, even on this dark night, I passed along the swamp going up the Wappoo Creek. We heard nothing of pursuit. At night it would have been impossible for them to follow us without the aid of dogs, which I presumed they would get as soon as possible.

Following the creek for about a mile and a half, we came upon a place where there was not more than three or four hundred yards of open ground to the Stono River. This was about half a mile above Fort Pemberton. Peering cautiously out of the undergrowth of the swamp in the direction of the river, we found no one moving and no guards set, the river above the fort being considered perfectly safe from any boat attack of the Federals. Crossing this ground hurriedly, we descended to the river, and there found a light skiff that Caucus had moored at the spot for this emergency. In it was a suit of decent clothing for me, and some simple but wholesome food, the first I had tasted for months. I immediately threw off the convict suit I wore, and donned the clothes while Caucus was pulling the skiff into mid-stream. In the pocket of the coat I found a loaded revolver.

"Who sent them for me, Caucus?" I whispered.

"Miss Laura. She's been tinkin' ob you and wringing her hands ober you for de las two days. She's had red eyes, sah; powerful red eyes, Massa Bryant."

These words added strength to a resolution I had already made.

While this was going on, Caucus had turned the boat down-stream and we were gliding toward the Federal gun-boats, some five miles distant. We had already reached a point in the river only a few hundred yards above Fort Pemberton.

"Where is your mistress?" whispered I.

"Miss Laura?"

"Certainly!"

"Oh, she's a mile or two up de ribber stopping wid Judge Elliott's family. Her brudder's stoppin' dar, too. He's looking after diggin' up some forts near heah. I's to go back and 'port to her when I's got you safe down de ribber to de Yanks."

"Very well," said I. "I must see her before I go. Turn the boat up-stream!"

"No, sah. I ain't nebber goin' up dis stream agin!"

"What do you mean?"

"I means when I gits to de Yanks I's a-gwine to stay dar. I's bound to be free like you is, sah."

"Then you are not going to return to your mistress?"

"No, sah. If I once get to de Yanks, I stays."

"Turn that boat up-stream! I must—I will see her before I go." I seized the tiller to change the direction of the little craft.

"Dis boat don't go up-stream wid me in it! I's gwine to be free!"

"Look here, Caucus," I said, "there's no use of your arguing with me or acting in that way;" for the black had raised his oar threateningly. "I am going up that river to see Laura Peyton, and you have got to go with me."

"Nebber!"

"Then I've got to go without you!" and I clapped my revolver to his head.

"You ain't gwine to kill me?" he gasped.

"Not if you do as I say, but if you make any disturbance here now, I will!"

By this time the boat had floated almost opposite the fort.

"If you want to get out, you can do so after we have got up-stream a little way, but we must go back first. It is too late to do anything else," I whispered, as I saw two patrol boats moving about down the river opposite the fort. "You see they know of our escape. We never could pass between them."

Fortunately during this conversation we had been

drifted by an eddy under the shadow of the bank and the patrol boats did not see us. The wind was blowing up-stream, and they could not hear us. Urged by my revolver, and perhaps by his fears, Caucus turned the boat about and rowed slowly up the river away from the Federal gunboats for which he longed.

"Look heah," he said, "it's sartin death for you to go up dar. If de rebs cotch you, whar am you?"

"I am going to see her before I go."

"Golly, you's gone mad, you has, sah! You dunno what you's doin'. If de rebs cotch you, you's a goner, and de Yankee gunboats ain't but few miles away, I reckon dey ain't so much, sah."

"Pull ahead!"

I cocked the revolver, and Caucus said no more for some time save an occasional ejaculation of "Fo' de Lord, you has gone crazy!" or some similar expression of astonished horror and disgust.

"Row quicker!" said I, sternly, whenever he relaxed his efforts, and in about an hour we rounded a bend in the stream upon the bank of which I could see lights, apparently from a house.

"Dat's de place, sah!"

"Where she is?"

"Yes, sah!"

As the boat drew up at the bank, I said, "Go into the house quickly, and tell her I am here. Don't you alarm the family, for the Elliotts are southerners to the backbone, and if this comes out, it means the whipping-post for you, as well as imprisonment for me."

"I knows dat, sah. Golly! I tink you treat pretty hard dis boy who helped you to 'scape."

"Tell her quickly," said I, "and when this is over, Caucus, I will make your disappointment up to you in some way. You know I was kind to you before. Be faithful to me, and I will be so again."

"All right, sah," said the volatile black, with a grin. "I's bound to get free dis trip, somehow, an' I s'pose I can put it off for a day or two."

With that he stole up one of the paths leading through the garden to a pretty cottage erected upon the banks of the stream, while I impatiently and anxiously placed myself in the shadow of some trees to wait as well as I could for the coming of the being for whom I had risked so much.

A few moments after this she was by my side with impatient words, almost reproaches. "For God's sake, Lawrence!—you may never escape now! Why didn't you go?"

"Because I love you."

"Yes; but think how unhappy you make me. If you are taken again, they will perhaps *kill* you!"

"To win you I would risk anything!"

"But you cannot win me if you die."

"I will win you *before!*"

"For heaven's sake, leave me! Take the boat and go down the river."

"That is an impossibility now," said I. "The Confederate patrol boats are on the alert. Every picket between here and the Federal lines knows that we have escaped," for at that moment I heard the booming of a gun down the river.

"You can go. You *must* go!"

"I will not go. I came here deliberately."

"And why?"

"To win you!"

"Win me!—what do you mean?"

"I mean this," said I. "If you love me, you would wish to save my life."

"I cannot save it if you do not leave South Carolina."

"I will never leave South Carolina until you are my wife. I made that resolution six months ago, when I was forced back into this State. Providence brought me back to be your husband."

"This is madness!"

"Laura, you must love me, after what you have done for me. For God's sake, do the only thing that will make me wish to save my life—*marry me now!*"

The astonished girl panted at this, and in a sort of desperate frenzy, I seized her in my arms and supplemented my peculiar wooing with all the kisses and endearments that I had hoarded up for the girl in my imagination during the long time I had been parted from her.

"For Heaven's sake have mercy upon me! Think of what my friends, my family, would say to my marrying you in this way."

"For my sake, have mercy upon me! Think of what my misery will be if I leave this place fearing I have lost you."

"We cannot be married to-night."

"Before I fly from South Carolina, we must be," I muttered, the sudden joy of knowing that I had won her coming to me with her words.

"For my sake, leave me! You will be captured! My heavens! they are coming now!"

The girl panted and clung to me while I listened, and through the darkness of the night heard the sound of cavalry and the clanking of sabers.

"Conceal yourself, for my sake!" she begged.

"Not unless you promise to be mine."

"And if not!"

"They'll find me here,—I don't care what becomes of me!"

"You are mad!"

"Yes, mad enough to do this."

"Quick! You won't have time,—let me hide you!"

"Do you promise?"

"YES! Anything to save your life! Come!"

She glided up the pathway. I followed her silently. I knew that I had conquered—that Laura Peyton's promise was her bond.

"This way!" She passed around one of the out-buildings, and coming to the barn, she led me into an old deserted portion of it, filled, as well as I could discover in the gloom, with rice seed and sacks for holding the same.

"Conceal yourself between these! I will send Caucus to look after you."

"By this kiss, remember your promise!"

She tore herself from me and left the place.

I could hear the Confederate soldiers outside questioning the family if they had seen about there a white escaped convict and a red-headed negro.

Next I heard Caucus' voice. "Golly, I 'specks I's de only red-headed nigger 'round dese parts!"

"Well," laughed the officer of the cavalry, "if you meet your twin brother, arrest him and we'll give a reward for him."

"How much reward?" said Caucus.

" Well, perhaps a hundred dollars."

" Say, you make it a thousand, and I'll delibber myself up for him," laughed Caucus, as the patrol rode away.

After a few minutes, the astonished exclamations and hearty laughter of the Elliotts at the wit of Caucus died away. I could tell from the voices that they were all women, young Arthur Peyton and the men of the house being off on duty at this time.

Half an hour or so after this Caucus came to me, but in a very surly mood, and gave me a very stale piece of corn bread and a by-no-means succulent sweet potato.

" Why didn't you bring better ? " asked I.

" Cuss you ! " replied Caucus. " Do you tink I's gwine to give you a good meal after you robbed me of my liberty ? What am I now ? A slabe ! But for yous I'd have been a free man an' a Caucussion ! Heah's someting else, sah ! " He handed me a scrap of paper.

" How am I to read this without any light ? "

" Come wid me ! "

I followed Caucus to an old cabin, perhaps two hundred yards from the house. It was near the bank of the river where our boat was moored. Here the negro soon lighted a tallow dip. By its light I saw Laura Peyton's well-remembered handwriting. It said :

" DARLING : I dare not visit you now, but will take the first opportunity as soon as the family are asleep—perhaps in half an hour. Was it not a little ungenerous, dear one, to take advantage of my fears for you ? Could you not see that it would have broken my heart if anything had happened to you ? That was the reason I gave you my promise ; but I will keep it if you will keep yours, and try to fly to safety."

If the delicate and maidenly reproach in the letter made me feel that I had not treated my sweetheart generously, the thought that I had won her obliterated it with joy.

A movement of the negro's attracted my attention. In the uncertain light I could see he still eyed me in a very sullen manner. I knew he had not forgiven me for bringing him back to slavery. If he betrayed me, there was an end to every hope.

" Caucus," said I, " you don't seem to like me as you used to."

" No, I's cussed if I does ! "

"Here's twenty dollars." I took this out of my hoard of greenbacks that Laura had returned to me.

"I don't want no money from you, Massa Bryant," he said, savagely, though he eyed the greenback in a greedy way.

"Oh, yes, you do, Caucus," said I; "you want it to hire a minister."

"*Hire a minister!* What for? To bury us when de rebs catch us?"

"No," I said, "to hire a minister to marry me."

"Marry you? Who you marry?"

"Can't you guess, Caucus?" said I.

"Golly! not Miss Laura? Dat's what you wanted to come back for?"

"Yes," I replied, "otherwise we would now both be free together. I have come back to marry your mistress."

"Fo' de Lord! Dat's what you brought me back for?" said Caucus, a grim smile lighting up his dusky features. "Well, den! If Miss Laura marries yous, I forgive yous. Great gosh! How de Peytons will cuss!" His grin changed into a guffaw.

"Then," replied I, "I will soon be in your good graces again. I will soon marry your mistress."

"Golly, dar's fun ahead ob us! Fo' de Lord, you's cute as a coon!" and the negro gave another wild chuckle.

I did not answer this. My thoughts had taken another turn. How was I to get a minister to make me the husband of Laura Peyton, unknown to her family, in a land where civil war made every one suspicious?

How was I, a fugitive, to do this?

CHAPTER XII.

THE HONEYMOON IN THE BLUE RIDGE.

THESE thoughts rapidly took my mind to my promised bride, her beauty, her love—now all mine again. For a moment I was in heaven. The next instant I was on earth. The negro's hand was on my arm. He muttered, "Hist!"

We both listened. Some one was apparently, from the noise, examining the boat that had brought us up the river.

"I'll see what dey's up to!" whispered Caucus, and he stole from the cabin, while I examined my revolver to be sure it was in condition for service.

With it, the forethought of my sweetheart had provided a little extra ammunition.

For fear the dampness had affected the priming, for some drops of water might have got on it when I had the trouble with Caucus on the river, I carefully placed a little fresh powder in each of its six nipples, and re-capped the cylinder. To do this I had to turn my back to the door in order to get the light from the candle.

I was just finishing this when I heard a chuckle, and looking over my shoulder, saw a man standing in the doorway of the cabin. To my sorrow, I recognized him. He was Pete Bassett, the Confederate detective.

"Wal!" remarked he, with a grin, "this is exhilarating as whisky! To meet you agin, Mister Bryant! I heard in Charleston four hours ago that you had cut out. Thar was a standing reward from a particular friend of yours to keep an eye on you, and I come after it."

"How did you discover me?" murmured I, capping the last nipple of the cylinder.

"Why, by instinct! I knew the gal was staying up har. I came and nosed around. I reckon'd if you tried to get down the river, our picket boats would have nipped you. So when I discovered that ar skiff had been out to-night and evacuated in a hurry by the oars left in it, I calculated I'd nabbed you again. So come along!" and he would have approached me.

"Stand where you are!"

"Not by a darned sight!"

'Stand!" I covered him with the cocked pistol.

"Crackey, I didn't know you were heeled!" He paused, astounded. Then he began: "Now, Mr. Bryant, you'd better take that thing down. You know you can't get out of this place, nohow. I'll go easy on you. I'll—if you put that cursed thing down—I'll let you go, I'll only take in that red-headed nigger! That'll stop the talk. Lord! won't they give it to that saffron-skulled darkey!" and the detective gave a hideous chuckle to try and throw me off my guard.

As he did so, a more hideous and awful chuckle came from behind him. Bassett's laugh closed with a gurgle. With a smothered cry, he fell senseless at my feet, and over him with a pick-handle that would have felled an ox stood Caucus.

"Wonder if dat smash his head in. Call me saffron skulled. D—n him!" and before I could interpose, another dreadful blow fell upon the head of the senseless Bassett.

I jumped forward and caught Caucus' upraised hand, and not without difficulty restrained him, for the negro's eyes had become bloodshot and his nostrils dilated with the scent of gore. The black was going back to his barbarous instincts. The meek slave was becoming like what he had sprung from, a Zulu warrior.

"What we does wid him?" he asked, showing his white teeth. "Finish him up, and chuck him in de ribber?"

"No, no; no murder!"

"If we not fix him, he fix us. His life or ours. If de rebs cotch us now, we's gwine in!"

"I know that, but I don't wish to kill him."

"He nearly dead now. It no hurt him. Why not? If we don't git him out ob de way, what become of us, Massa Bryant?"

"That's true," I replied. "We will get him out of the way, and I'll show you how." For an idea had just come to me by which we might be relieved of the presence of Mr. Bassett. "We'll take most of his clothes off; he'll hardly be known by the rest if the rebels pick him up. I suppose none of the pickets down at Fort Pemberton know him personally. If they do, he won't be in a condition to tell 'em anything, for a week or so. If he gets past them, the Federal gunboats 'll take care of him to the end of the war."

"What you mean to do?" asked the black eagerly, for I had already pulled the coat and vest off Mr. Bassett, and was examining his linen. This I was relieved to find was in no very good shape, as regards either cleanliness or condition, and bore no marks by which he could be recognized.

"I'm going to put him adrift in the skiff. He'll float down the river. If the rebs pick him up they won't know him, and if he gets to the Union boats he can't hurt any one."

"Dat's good, Massa Bryant!" muttered the negro with a grin. "Hope he'll get to de sharks and 'gators, or de Yankee gunships. Call me sarsafras-skulled niggah—cuss him!"

With that, aided by me, he dragged the insensible Bassett to the boat, and, propelled by a vigorous push, the skiff with its load floated down the stream.

As we did so, however, Bassett gave a low groan, and this was echoed by a female voice beside me. I turned hurriedly, and Laura Peyton, with a pale face, gasped tremblingly to me: "Lawrence—you—you have killed some one?"

"Not exactly, darling," I replied, taking her in my arms and trying to comfort her. "But I've been fixing a man who stood between me and liberty and you!"

With this I told her hurriedly of Mr. Bassett's commission from Amos Pierson, and what Caucus and I had done to the detective.

"This complicates matters fearfully," she returned, after a pause of consideration. "Come what may, Lawrence, I'm glad you did not kill him. Now that this has happened, you must get away from here instantly."

"Not until you keep your promise!"

"How can I keep my promise? Who can marry us here? You act like a crazy man," she muttered, wringing her hands.

"Until you are my wife, I make no attempt to leave South Carolina. I won't exist with the fear of losing you to make my life the miserable one it has been these last six months."

"Whether you leave South Carolina or not, you must fly from here to-night!"

"Not without hope!" said I, doggedly.

"You must!"

"NOT WITHOUT HOPE!"

"Well, then," said she, "you stubborn one, I'll give you hope!"

"How?"

"Let me think," she muttered, knitting her brows.

"Let me think!" And for a minute she remained motionless, except that a silent tear or two ran down her cheeks.

Then she cried suddenly, a look of resolution beaming in her eye : "Listen to me, Lawrence Bryant, and remember, in all the life we may go through together, what I do for love of you now. Like most men you love—a little selfishly—that doesn't make us women love less, so long as you love us. Now in your selfishness you threaten a practical suicide, unless I do what you demand—a thing that will separate me from the love of my family. But why should I go over this again? I, because your death would break my heart, have consented to this."

"No, no!" I cried. "Laura, forgive me!" for her generosity brought my selfishness home to me. "You shall not sacrifice yourself for my mad passion. I'll, for your sake, try and save myself—try and escape to the North. And when this awful struggle is ended, if we both live, I'll come back to you."

"Come back to me perhaps after half a century. Who knows how long this war may continue? Do they fight any the less now that so many are killed—that there are so many widows and orphans, and each day makes more? No, Lawrence—" here she beamed on me—"I'll not take the chance of losing, neither. I'm glad now that you fought for *our* happiness. I'll marry you, come what may, as I promised. You wouldn't have me break my word to you, would you, dear one?" this last with a pitiful smile that contained two tears.

"You'll marry me?" I cried.

"As soon as possible!"

"How?"

"A-a-h. How?" She gave another sigh, and thought hard again. Then said, "I'll tell you how!" speaking with sudden determination. "There is a part of this State so blessed by God that this cruel war has never reached it. Far away to the northwest, cut off by the high peaks of the Blue Ridge and Alleghany from the awful carnage and bloodshed of Tennessee, and too far from the coast to be engulfed in the cruel devastation that is scourging the country about here, the pretty mountains and upland valleys of Spartanburg

7

county, save for the absence of their sons, hardly know
of the carnage that is going on all round them. My
aunt, Miss Mary Pickens, has a little farm near the
boundary of North Carolina, not far from Jackson Hill.
She is an old lady of about seventy, and has lived there as
long as I can recollect, waited upon and tended by two
negroes, who are as old as herself. She is bright and active
for a woman of her years, and would be sure to discover
the circumstances that brought us to her, but, fortunately,
I being her favorite niece, received a letter from her not
long ago stating that she was going to make a visit to her
sister, in Augusta, Georgia. The old cook is the only one
left in the house. She adores me, and will believe anything I tell her. In that portion of the State you would be
unknown, and would be as safe as it is possible for you to
be in the Confederacy. Meet me there, and I will keep
my promise."

"You will marry me there?"

"Y-e-s!" she replied, slowly, with a sigh, then giving me a slight smile, murmured: "It is near 'The
Land of the Sky.' Lawrence, in happier days, I would
have picked it out for—a—a honeymoon in the Blue
Ridge," the last with a blush that looked crimson in
the light of the candle.

"You will meet me there?"

"Certainly. Come to my aunt's house." And she
gave me careful directions. "Four days from now I
will be there. I can easily make the excuse of visiting
my aunt to my father, brother, and sister, who do not
know that she is absent from her mountain home.——
But how to get there?" At this she paused, and then
cried despairingly, "This war has made me so very
poor!" The next moment, covering her face with her
hands, she muttered: "I should not have told this *to
you!*"

"Darling," said I, "why did you not use the money
that I sent to you six months ago?"

There was a little reproach in my tone, for during
this interview, I had been looking at the plain homespun
dress of my sweetheart, the coarse shoes, and the
absence of all the little delicate adornments which she
had been used to wear in the happier days of our first
engagement. "Why didn't you spend the money?"

" I could not take it from *you*, when I supposed you would not be my husband," she cried. " Oh, I am so glad now that I have been able to return it to you intact, without having touched a dollar of it ! "

" So am I," replied I. " Fate made you save it. It gives us money enough to make *the attempt* to become happy."

With this, after much entreaty, I forced upon her a sufficient amount for all the requirements of her journey.

" Why," she said, "this almost makes me feel rich. Every dollar of this is worth twenty of Confederate money. But how are you to get away? That is the real difficulty. Without a pass you can travel nowhere in this portion of the State."

At this I began to think. How was I to leave the neighborhood of Charleston without a passport? Every train was guarded, and every traveler without papers looked upon with suspicion. This obstacle to our plans would have appeared insurmountable had not, at this moment, my eye rested upon the coat and vest of the detective. Filled with a new hope, I seized Bassett's clothes and thoroughly searched them. In them I found a pocket-book full of papers and money, which I thought best to take with me ; also a passport made out to travel on business of importance to the Confederate Government. It was a general, unlimited, roving kind of passport, though, unfortunately, it gave a description of Mr. Bassett with which I did not thoroughly agree, though our height and weight were about the same.

" I must try it with these papers," said I. " They are my only chance. Let Caucus guide me to the railroad, in order that I may get a train for Columbia, thence on to Spartanburg. Then he can return and bring you to me."

I hurriedly asked her if the schedule time of the South Carolina Railroad had been altered in the last six months. She said she thought that it had not. If this was so, I knew the running time, and could make my arrangements accordingly. In order to catch the early train, it was necessary for me to start at once. I called Caucus, explained the matter to him, and he agreed to what I said. He remarked that there wouldn't be any danger for himself in traveling with a young lady as well known as Miss Peyton, and he could get along very well without me, as I had only been a source of danger to him ever since he had met me.

We were all too much excited to make my parting with my sweetheart a tearful or a sad one. We had not time to think.

Leaving her ; under the guidance of Caucus, who knew the by-ways of this part of the country thoroughly, I traveled rapidly north from the Stono River, crossing the Charleston and Savannah Railroad track, and taking a small country road, succeeded in reaching the Seven-Mile station on the South Carolina Railroad. This was just sufficiently outside the picket lines of the Confederates around Charleston to be safe.

Sending Caucus back to my sweetheart, with strict injunctions to watch over her until I met them, I boarded the train, muffled myself up well about the head, and pretended to sleep, in order to avoid interrogations.

The running time of all trains upon the railroad was now so bad, owing to their defective tracks, that I knew it would probably be evening before we reached Columbia. This suited me very well, as there was less chance of my being recognized in that town at night. The hardships and trouble I had been through had, to a certain extent, altered me, and the poor clothes I now wore, so different to my apparel of a few months ago, made the change in me a great one. Another thing in favor of my not being recognized was that the exigencies of the war had called all the young men away to the army ; consequently the former brakemen and conductors had been removed, and their places taken by old men, who had not seen me in my railroad position, and did not know me. It was night when we reached Columbia. My ticket was taken up and my pass examined by the last conductor. Among the things I had found in the pocket of the detective's coat was a plug of tobacco. In my haste I had transferred it to mine. This was fortunate, as I was just about to leave the train when the conductor suddenly turned to me and said : " Can you favor me with a chaw, Mr. Bassett ? "

" A what ? "

" A chaw of tobacco, of course. "

I put my hand in my pocket and found the plug.   Had

I not been able to do so, the conductor might have suspected me. I presume he knew Mr. Bassett's habits, and that he never traveled without his tobacco.

Leaving the train, and going into an out-of-the-way portion of the town, where I would be apt to meet no one who would recognize me, I spent most of the night. The next morning I sent a negro to buy my ticket, for I was afraid that the ticket-seller would remember me. Having procured this, the early train took me up into the hills.

I now felt more at my ease. Every mile I went, carried me away not only from the scene of war, but from the people whom I had known, and who might recognize me. That evening I put up at the little country hotel of Spartanburg, the landlady of which was a widow, her husband having been killed at Gettysburg.

Here I waited—waited impatiently for two long days, most of the time watching the road leading north from Spartanburg, for I knew that along this my sweetheart must pass to the place where she had promised to be my bride. The beautiful country about me, the bracing atmosphere of these hills, so different to the clammy moisture of the swamp country of the coast where I had toiled, all were naught to me—I looked only for her. I did not see her, but the evening of the second day the landlady said that Miss Peyton had hired a wagon from her to go out to her Aunt Mary's place. That night I hardly slept. The next morning I drove out toward Cowpens Ford, and turning up a little mountain road, an 'hour afterward, Mr. Caucus, with an exclamation of delight and a horrible grin, opening the gate for me, I was in the arms of my sweetheart once more.

" Did I not keep my promise?" she said. "Did I not? But oh! how I had to fib to my family. What deception! I almost despise myself for it. I wonder if they will ever forgive me. My poor father!"

She commenced to wring her hands, and would have gone on in this style had not I, inspired by her presence said : "Laura, this is no time for tears. We must be married at once."

"At once?" this with a little tremble.

"Immediately!" I returned. "Were we to be met together, your situation would now be embarrassing."

"Oh, I had forgotten that!" she cried, giving me a delicious blush. "Old Mr. Huntington, the minister who baptized me, lives not two miles from here. He is both a little deaf and a little blind, but I imagine a ceremony performed by him will be as binding as if solemnized by a minister with the complete use of his faculties. Will you ride over to him and give him this note from me? I think he remembers me as a child."

I soon found the old preacher, and two hours afterward returned with him. Here a new rapture awaited me. Laura swept into the room. In some occult manner, in Columbia, she had obtained a white muslin dress and a little French ribbon, perhaps the relic of her finery before the war. Radiant with blushes and love, my bride was a perfect goddess of beauty.

The marriage ceremony between us was performed. Half an hour afterward the minister drove away, and my bride and I strolled out on the veranda of the old house. Behind us were the beautiful peaks of the Alleghany and Blue Ridge, that cut off the desolation of war from us. Below, a hundred beautiful little hills gradually rolled into the valleys that ran down to the sea-coast, red with the blood of civil contest. ·

In this fair country, divorced by nature from the passions of men, we had only to live for each other now and be happy while God would let us. For a month we tried to live the life of forgetfulness, and in part succeeded. What man would not think that Heaven intended his fate to be happy, blessed as I was by the supreme love and beauty that my wife gave to me? But still neither of us could forget the danger that surrounded us. This made us very cautious, and actuated by this, my wife wrote several letters to her family describing the happy visit she was making her aunt.

It was a curious honeymoon. The sudden opening of a door caused the bride to start; a step upon the piazza or on the walk outside made the bridegroom handle his pistol. The faithful Caucus, however, was always on the alert, and nearly every day went down to Spartanburg to get the news; but no troops were moving in this country, which had been denuded of all its young men, and we were far enough away from the great highways to the gaps of the Blue Ridge by which reinforcements were sent into the valley of the Tennessee to be rid of marching troops. We lulled ourselves into a hope that this might last forever, until, one clear winter's day, the sword descended—our honeymoon in the Blue Ridge ceased forever. Like most tragedies, it came unexpectedly.

CHAPTER XIII.

WHEN GIRL MEETS GIRL!

THE day had been one of dreamy happiness. We had now almost deluded ourselves with the hope that a happier Providence than that which had heretofore been over us would still permit us to linger in each other's love, despite the whirl of war around us. The day had been one worthy of the superb scenery about us that gave a tinge of poetic romance to our love. We had been sitting together on the veranda, looking down the slopes of the Blue Ridge, upon which a little stream ran toward the plains upon which the war raged that we had grown now to look upon as very distant. Behind us the mountains rose into the blue air, and were covered with a slight snow, for it was late in December.

"Laura," said I, giving her slight waist a little honeymoon squeeze, "do you remember this day three years ago? The night of the little dance at your house—the day Secession was declared?"

"Yes, Lawrence," she muttered, "I have never forgotten that; but please do not at this moment mention what reminds me of the last three terrible years. Here, cut off from bloodshed and trouble by that little range of hills below, let us be happy while we can; the time will be too short.——My heavens! whose voice is that?"

At this she turned pale and began to tremble nervously, and I turned pale also, for—"This is Aunt Mary's house, I reckon, isn't it, Caucus?" came to us in the accents of the woman I wished least to meet on earth—Miss Belle Peyton, Laura's sister.

I could hear the negro's teeth chatter; next his voice

came to me in a kind of grinning yell : " Golly gracious !
Miss Belle's heah !   Miss Belle's heah !   'Clare to goodness, Miss Belle's heah ! "

He ran about the garden shrieking this out, apparently
to give us warning.

" Are you crazy, Caucus ?   Open the gate at once, and
let me in ! " said Belle, hurriedly.

The next moment she rode into the garden.   Pale, but
firm, Laura rose to meet her sister.

I can see Belle now as she came running up the steps,
crying : " Laura, I grew anxious about you when Aunt Mary
wrote me from Augusta saying nothing of you.   I thought
it curious that you were making her a visit when she was
not at home.   But now I will stay a week or two with
you myself.   We'll have a delightful time up in these lovely
hills.   We'll——Oh ! my soul !   *This* is the cause of your
visit.   You are staying here with this man.   My sister,
what does it mean ? " and Belle glared at me with fiery
eyes.

At this Laura said, very calmly, though there was a tremble in her voice, " Belle, let me introduce to you my
husband, Mr. Lawrence Bryant."

" *Your husband ?* " shrieked Belle.   " Oh, heavens ! this
is worse than I feared ! "

" My husband, whom I love and honor, and whom you
must respect, Belle, if we are to be sisters."

" *Sisters ?* When you have married one of our enemies ?
This man who loved the North so much that he left you
to fly to it ?   Oh, what degradation !   What misery !
What despair !   What will my poor old father say to—
this ? " and the girl began to pant with passionate rage
and hysterical misery.

" He will say nothing.   You must not tell him—at
present," came from Laura's pale but resolute lips.

" But I *will* tell him, so that he can despise you as I
do.   Loving this man who would destroy us—a YANKEE."
This last was uttered as if it was a term of contempt
beyond anything else on earth.   " A YANKEE ! "

The girl came toward me with flashing eyes, looking
as if she would almost attack me.

" Oh, how I hate you ! " she hissed.   " You who have
lured my sister away from her duty and her friends.   A
man who had not heart enough to fight us, but must

destroy our family by making a woman love him, and she—my sister," and she burst out crying, sobbing, and wringing her hands.

I had said nothing to this, judging it best to let her exhaust her childish fury. Now I remarked: " Miss Belle, I loved your sister before this war came to separate us. You used to like me then; can you not think a little kindly of one who regards you as—a sister?"

"Your *sister?* she shrieked. "I will not be your sister *long*. I have heard that you are a criminal—a deserter from the ranks of our army twice over. Good-by, Laura! Your honeymoon will be a short one."

The girl turned to go, and almost staggered while doing so.

"What do you mean?" cried Laura, suddenly confronting her. "Where are you going?"

"I am going to the nearest military post to denounce this man you have wed, and to deliver him up to our authorities, that he may be shot to death. That's what they'll do to him! Then he can call me 'sister' no more. Then our disgrace may be wiped out by his blood. You shall be his widow—not his wife!"

"You will do nothing of the kind," said Laura, very calmly. "You are crazy now, Belle. You will stay here until your mania is over."

"I will stay here not a second! Don't you try to detain me! Keep your hands off me!" for Laura had placed a detaining grasp on Belle's arm. "How dare you?"

"It is my duty," said Laura, "to my husband and to you to stop an insane woman from doing what she would regret forever. Do you suppose I will let you, in your mad anger, murder the man I love? Do you think that I am crazy as well as you? You will stay here until you regain your sanity!"

"Not another second under the roof that is polluted by this man. Oh, my Heaven, Laura! how could you do it? But I will do my duty, if you forget yours, you renegade!" The two girls stood confronting each other, the dark eyes of one flashing anger into the resolution in the blue eyes of the other.

"Lawrence," returned Laura, calmly, "give me your

assistance. Your life depends on it. This girl is mad enough to do what she promises!"

I saw that my only chance of safety was in obeying my wife's request. I came, and as tenderly as possible took hold of Belle's arm.

"Oh, you're a northern gentleman!" she hissed, "to lay your hands on a woman! It is like you Yankees!"

"Belle, stop these insults," cried Laura, "or I shall forget that you are my sister! *Stop them!* Lawrence, *Quick!*" for Belle had commenced to struggle and scream in her hysterical rage.

Then Laura and I, as delicately and tenderly as was possible, drew the struggling girl into the house, and securely locked her into one of the upper rooms.

This apartment was a kind of attic, the windows of which were protected by iron bars from the assaults of negro thieves, the place being used as a family storeroom. I shall never forget the look in that girl's eyes that fell on me as we left her! The rage of "a tigress robbed of her young" would do no justice to the picture that Miss Belle's pretty face made as we closed the door on her and turned the key in the padlock.

Laura and I descended the stairs, despair in our hearts. We knew our honeymoon was over, that the war had drifted from the plains of South Carolina into this quiet valley of the Blue Ridge.

"Lawrence, we must part now. There is but one place of safety for you, and that is on the other side of the line."

"Now?" I muttered.

"Yes; I know you would stay with me. You would risk your life for my happiness, for another day with me; but you must go. It may be a sweetheart's wish to detain her husband. It is a wife's duty to bid him Godspeed at such a time as this."

"Laura, you must go with me!"

"I cannot! I dare not! I must keep this girl here, or you will be pursued before you can reach any place of safety. I will join you in the North. It will not be difficult for me to take passage in a blockade-runner. Women are non-combatants. I will meet you wherever you tell me. My life here could hardly be pleasant now; with you away from me it would be misery. I shall keep Belle securely, but tenderly, until the danger of her denouncing you is passed."

After this I did not attempt to persuade my wife to accompany me upon the hazardous journey I was about to undertake. I had long ago mapped out the route I should take on leaving the Confederacy. It was across the State line, but a few miles distant, into North Carolina, then through the western portion of that State into the mountains of East Tennessee, entering the Union lines near Knoxville.

Dangerous as this road was, on account of guerillas, bushwhackers, and scouts, it was the best now open to me.

I made my preparations hurriedly, silently, with almost a broken heart. That night my wife and I parted. Our honeymoon ended almost as suddenly as it had begun, but I left with the joy that now she was mine ; no other suitors could rob me of her. She was not my sweetheart—she was my wife.

This journey I was to make alone. I would not take even Caucus with me, as it was necessary that he should stay by my wife. I was thoroughly armed with a pair of navy revolvers, had a fairly good horse, and fifty dollars in greenbacks in my pocket. The balance of my hoard I left with Laura for any expenses and emergencies she might meet with and to pay her passage on some blockade-runner to Nassau, thence to New York.

As Caucus opened the gate of the garden, and bade me good-by, I could see the pale, distracted face of my wife, as she stood in the doorway of the house. I did not dare look back too long, and, setting my teeth, turned my head away to make my escape, for her sake as well as my own.

My preparations had occupied me till perhaps nine o'clock at night. Beyond the gate of the garden, my road ran down a little lane lined with laurel trees. The moonlight, however, reflected from the snow of the neighboring hills, made this lane quite light. I was leaning on my horse, arranging the articles that I carried with me in a knapsack slung upon the saddle, when I heard these words, that gave me a terrible start : " By Gosh ! I've got you now, and this time you don't escape me ! "

Glancing hurriedly up, I saw confronting me, not ten feet away, the form of Pete Bassett, who had me covered with a revolver.

Fortunately one of my pistols was in a holster hanging from the saddle, and my hand rested upon it. I did not move it as I knew that any motion would be the signal for my death, but with a presence of mind born of the situation, I said quietly : " Mr. Bassett, I never expected to see you again."

" No," he replied. " And you don't like it, after having that nigger beat me nearly to death, and then shipping me down the river in a boat, delirious for two weeks, so I could not give an account of myself. You didn't reckon on me to find you agin, but that reward is still open from that particular friend of yours. So I come up and nosed around Columbia, and when I saw your gal's sister Belle start out suddenly for this part of the State, I followed her, and having got a glimpse of the gal you are sweet on through the window of that house, I knew you wasn't far away. Now I have got you sure ! You don't dodge me agin. Throw up your hands ! "

" Yes, I do ! " cried I, with a laugh. " Hit him again, Caucus ! "

With an oath the detective suddenly wheeled and faced about to confront, as he supposed, the negro once more. As he did so my hand drew my pistol from its holster, and like lightning I shot him, for I had no mercy now. This man had three times stepped between me and escape, and I knew if I did not kill him there would be but little chance for me.

With a horrid yell, Bassett fell into the roadway. I stepped up to him and he gasped : "Played me agin, Gol darn it ! and this time played out forever ! Fust laid out by a nigger, and then chawed up by a Yank ! "

With this he fainted, probably with disgust, as his hurt did not seem to be mortal.

As I bent down over the wounded man, Caucus and my wife, attracted by the noise of the shooting, came running down the avenue. From her appearance I am sure that Laura thought I had been the victim, for she gave a sigh of relief when she saw me standing erect.

" What new horror is this?" she gasped, while Caucus gave a grin and chuckled : " You fixed him dis time didn't you, Massa Bryant ? An' I fixed him de last time ! I reckon we got to bury him dis time ! "

" That would not trouble me much," I replied. " He has had three chances at my liberty—now I have had one chance at his life ! "

" Lawrence, you must not stay here ! " said my wife. " We will do what we can for this wounded man. Go on at once, you may be pursued ! This has made your flight even more imperative than Belle's visit ! "

Another hurried parting, another last kiss, and I started once more upon my journey.

BOOK IV.

How I Came Back and Fought for Her.

CHAPTER XIV.

INTO THE DARK COUNTRY.

I HAD made up my mind to follow the road which led across the State line into Henderson County, thence to Asheville, in Buncombe County, and the French Broad River, which would give me a direct route through one of the gaps of the Blue Ridge and Alleghany Mountains into East Tennessee. Now, fearing immediate pursuit, I whispered my change of plans to my wife. I determined to go somewhat off the direct route by way of Rutherford County, which would probably throw any people following me off my track. Taking a few hurried directions from her lips, for Laura knew the country very well, I took the small road leading across the State line to Island Ford, in Rutherford County, North Carolina.

It was only a few miles distant, and in about an hour and a half, by riding rapidly, I had made the place. From here I passed rapidly along to Rutherfordton, a little village and county-seat, arriving there some time after midnight. From this place, after resting my horse, I followed the directions given me, and about three in the morning reached Green's Hill. The country was very thinly settled, and that night I was disturbed by nothing save the barking of a few curs as I passed along near the farm-houses on the road.

I was approaching Green's Hill when I heard the clatter

of a horse's hoofs behind me. Urging my tired beast to his speed, I kept along as rapidly as possible, but in spite of me, the sound came nearer and nearer. Fearing that I was pursued, and knowing that it was by only one man, for I could hear only the noise of one horse, I drew up in the shade of some trees to let him pass me, or to see what he intended to do.

I had not been in this position more than a minute or two when a form of a man on horseback rapidly passed me. By the uncertain light, it seemed familiar to me.

I hallooed, " Is that you, Caucus ? "

" Golly ! Fo' de Lord, Massa Bryant ! I came near passin' you ! You come right along wid me. Dey is fixin' up a party to pursue you down dar in Spartanburg. Dey ain't half an hour behind me. Miss Laura said I was to come along to tell you. Dis note's from her, and 'll give you all de statistic. Come along with me, quick ! "

Together we spurred along the road to beyond Green's Hill; then turning to the north, under Caucus' direction, who had been through this country before, we followed a little mountain path until we reached the stream called Otter Creek, which I believe connects with the French Broad River further on. The country here was very wild, and our horses were quite tired, though they were fresh when we started, we having ridden over thirty miles that night

As soon as morning came, we turned from the road into the bushes, where we could hardly be discovered, made a fire, and after eating a breakfast which I had brought with me (though Caucus had brought a much more elaborate meal with him), and tethering the horses, we lay down to rest.

I was so worn out that it was long after mid-day when I awoke with a start of misery. The negro snored contentedly by my side ; the horses, a little way off, browsed upon the grass about them. What had happened to me ? I knew some sorrow had overtaken me. After a moment the scene brought my loss home to me. My wife, my companion, my sweetheart, was parted from me, perhaps forever !

This recalled to me the note that Caucus had brought from her. The light had been too dim to read it when slumber fell upon me.   I hurriedly tore open the epistle. It read as follows :

"MONDAY EVENING.

"MY DARLING HUSBAND : I send these hurried lines to warn you that a party is being collected to pursue you.   This ought to reach you about an hour ahead of them.   They can hardly take the road before that time has passed.   Your pistol shot attracted some men riding along the road.   Bassett was able to tell them, and direct their movements.   Thank God, my sister Belle had no hand in putting these bloodhounds on your track.   Oh, my darling Lawrence, how I shall pray for you to-night !   Bereft of your presence, I feel like a widow now—that these are a widow's tears that fall upon this paper. Guard your life, for it is my life, my husband !   God grant that we may meet again, is the one prayer that will go up to heaven, my own, my darling one, from your loving, despairing wife,

"LAURA PEYTON BRYANT.

"I sign my new name, dearest, for the first time.   Oh ! God protect you !   L."

I had seen the dear handwriting many times before, but never had it despair in it like this, the first, perhaps the last note I should ever receive from my wife.

My eyes filled with tears as I cursed my selfish passion that had caused this beautiful creature to risk her happiness on the existence of the hunted creature that I now was.   As I re-read the letter, and the significance of the words, "Guard *your* life—for it is *my* life, my husband !" came fully to me, I determined to use a circumspection, forethought, and prudence in my movements through the dark and bloody land of the guerilla and bushwhacker I was now coming to, that for my own sake I should hardly have contemplated.

I awakened the negro with some difficulty.   At first he seemed astonished, but after a moment recollected, and said, "Fo' de Lord ! at first I reckoned I was out coon huntin', Massa Bryant, but now I 'members dat you an me is de coons, an' somebody else is de hunters."

I directed Caucus to get us something to eat, which he did very quickly, as we thought it safer to make no fire and eat some of what was already cooked in our knapsacks.

While we were doing this I questioned Caucus, and learned that there were probably about six men in the party pursuing us ; that he knew the country quite well, having hunted over it when living with Laura's aunt years before; his acquaintance with the country roads and

topography of the neighborhood going pretty accurately
as far as the boundaries of Yancey County, about twenty
miles from where we were. Beyond that point his knowledge was vague, uncertain and muddled.

I had a general idea of the main lines of travel to the
gaps in the Blue Ridge myself, and pondered long upon
the route I should take. At first I thought of going
directly west *via* Asheville into Tennessee ; but that
would place me well south of the Union lines between
Knoxville and Chattanooga, and every highway between
those two places was filled with detachments of Confederate soldiers. I abandoned, but reluctantly, the
route *via* Asheville, as it was much the more direct and
easier to travel. Had I not done so, the information
that Caucus brought me from the road over which we
had come the night before would have caused me to
abandon the Asheville route. For while I was pondering
the black had sneaked cautiously down to the highway,
from which he returned in a state of great excitement.

" Great gosh ! Dey's on our scent, Massa Bryant," he
said.

" Who ? "

" Dem Home Guardians from Spartanburg."

" Home Guards. How do you know that ? "

" Seed der tracks—seed 'em in de road—de marks of
der hosses."

" What makes you think they are from Spartanburg ? "

" Seed de off fore shoe of de horse Miss Belle rode
yesterday—it war broken. One ob dem fellahs took
Belle's horse to ride last night, and dar's de print of a
broken off fore shoe in de road in front ob us. Reckon
dey's gone on to Marion to rouse 'em up to look for us."

" How many were they ? "

" Three, sah ! "

" I thought you said the party of Home Guards num-
bered six ? "

" So I did, sah. Reckon de oders of dem went off de
Asheville road to gibe us a deal if we come out dat way.
I don't feel quite comfortable, sah ! "

" Neither do I, Caucus," I replied, as I saw another
avenue of escape cut off, that by Marion—the main town
of McDowell County, in which we now were.

" Look here, Cauk," said I, " do you know any by-

path or mountain road leading from here north, between
Asheville and Marion ? "

" Yes, sah.   One by Three Forks."

" Where's that ? "

" About twenty miles from heah, on de borders of
Yancey County."

" And after that do you know the way to the north ? "

" No, sah ; but I's heerd folks speak about it.   Dar's
a place called Mitchell."

" Any gap to go through the mountains into Tennessee ? "

" Don't know, sah.   Reckon dar is.   Dar's a riber up
dar called de 'Chuckey."

" You mean the Nolachucky, don't you ? "

" Don't know, sah.   I neber heard it called nothin' but
de 'Chuckey."

" Very well," said I, after some thought.   " We'll go
to Three Forks to-night," for I had already made up my
mind to try and get through into Mitchell, a border
county of North Carolina on the Blue Ridge, and then
by going almost due west through the mountains into
East Tennessee, I should strike Knoxville.

" Better not start till dark, sah," remarked Caucus.
" Might meet dose Home Guardians on de back track."

" Can you find the way at night ? "

" Sure, Massa Bryant."

" Very well, then ; we'll leave at dusk."

This we accordingly did after making our supper without lighting a fire, as the forethought of my wife had
given me cooked provisions to last me several days, and
Caucus had taken a good stock for himself when he left
in pursuit of me.

I placed the precious letter from my darling Laura
along with the few papers I carried with me, among them
the passport belonging to the detective, Bassett.   This
might be of use to me in case of detention by Confederate scouts.

I knew that we were now approaching rapidly the border country where some were Secessionists and others
Union people, and that with each step we took our danger from bushwhackers and scouts increased.   We had
more evidences of this as we progressed.   A burnt cabin
by the roadside, a destroyed corn-crib, and the manner

in which a man we met in the road took to the woods
all showed me that we were gradually getting into the
bloody ground of western North Carolina and East Tennessee, where neighbor fought with neighbor and brother
slew brother.

Soon after starting we turned to the north, leaving
Marion on our right, and I gave a sigh of relief as Caucus informed me that he "reckoned that we had now left
de road where de Home Guardians might come back on
us."

I knew in case of detention by Confederate troops that
I must have some definite object in my journey, and determined to be traveling about buying up mules for the
Confederate army. I explained this to Caucus, telling
him he must pass as my servant; and as we rode along
asked him, as there were a good many Union men in this
part of the State, if he could not recollect, in his experience here before the war, some one that he thought
would now be true to the Old Flag.

"Yes sirree! I's takin' you to one now—up at Three
Forks."

"What makes you think he is a Unionist?"

"Wall, he comed down heah when he war a boy, sah,
and dough he's trapped and hunted in de mountains
heah for thirty or forty years, dey always call him afore
de war 'Ole Yank.' Reckon he must be Ole Yank
still, sah."

"Perhaps so," returned I. "We'll try Old Yank, anyway. I like the sound of the name."

We traveled on till nearly morning over some very
rough country, for Caucus took us by every out-of-the-
way path he could think of, and after having gone
nearly twenty-five miles, as near as I could judge, the
black announced that he reckoned we was "nigh onto
Three Forks."

As the morning advanced and the light became
stronger, Caucus began to look about anxiously, and
muttered:

"Can't be possible I comed wrong!" Then suddenly
cried: "Crackey, I knowed I was right, Massa Bryant.
Why dar's Ole Yank's dorg, wid de cut-off tail. Hi,
Badger!" This last to a snarling hound, who came running out of a farm-yard to bark at us.

At sight of us, a girl coming out with a milk pail in her hand hurriedly reëntered the house, and a moment after "Ole Yank" himself, gun in hand, confronted us as we came up to his front door.

"Why, dar's de ole man hisself. 'Clare to goodness, Mister Yank, I was skeered you war dead! Don't you 'member Cauk—dat used to carry de grub for you out huntin'?"

"Wall!" said the old gentleman. "I guess I do—never forgot that h'ar of yourn. Dreamt of it one night, —woke up, and found my hay-rick on fire. What brings you up here? These aren't no good times to travel." And the old man looked suspiciously at me.

From the moment he used the word "guess," I felt pretty sure he came from the North.

"That's a rather dangerous title the people give you about here," I said, to test my idea.

"Yas, they've called me Ole Yank, 'fore the war, and I sticks up for the name now. Have you anything to say agin it?" Here he looked significantly at his gun.

"No!" replied I, "but I want to speak to you," and without more ado I told him the truth about myself.

"Come right in here, I likes to look at fellows like you!" He grabbed my hand, ushered us into the house and cried out: "Gals, get a right smart breakfast for this gentleman!"

His daughters, three comely, bright-eyed, lithe but buxom mountain maidens, sprang to do his bidding, for "Old Yank" was an autocrat in his house.

After breakfast I explained my plans to him, and he said: "You stay here till to-morrow morning. You'll need a rest before you tackle the job ahead of you, for it's a powerful nasty one. I'll think over your matter, and give you a leetle good advice."

To this I readily consented. I explained my position and plans to him, and he answered me in about these words:

"To most men I'd say go back—to you I says go ahead, sonny, it's your only chance. From here on every step you take becomes more dangerous. But Lord! boys like you has to take some chances. Now I'll help you all I kin. You'd better light out early to-morrow morning to Tittle's place. It's about four hours' travel north of here, on the borders of Mitchell County. Give him this grip," here he seized my hand. "He'll return it so," with this he grabbed me again. "Then he'll tell you what you'd better do next. Remember that grip, my lad; the man that can't return it to you in these parts, look out for, and git ready to have the drop on him. Take a paper and make yourself comfortable, while I do the chores."

He handed me the *Raleigh Weekly Standard*, the office of which was afterward demolished by a mob of Confederates. We passed a very comfortable day here, Caucus looking after our horses.

After supper in the evening, the girls drew around the fire, together with the old gentleman, who amused us with anecdotes of his early life in the mountains and some original remarks upon the war.

Then one of the girls said: "Dad, suppose some of the rebs come here to-night, what will you do with this gentleman? You know they don't like you any too well, and I think you ought to have some plan to guard against any surprise in the middle of the night."

"Wall," said Old Yank, "they do come round here quite often. They seem to have a grudge agin me. P'raps it's fur my name; but then I allus manage to git along without much trouble. Why, one night half a dozen of them fellers came ridin' up here an' said they'd come fur me, an' I'd have to go into the army; but I jest reached 'round the door and pulled out my Henry rifle, an' my gals understood it an' got their double-barreled shotguns, an' I jest told them boys I had lived too long in the mountains to be scared that way, an' if they wanted to stop in my house they was welcome, but if they laid hands on an ole man like me they'd never do it agin, fur my gals had the bead on 'em. One of 'em said they didn't want any trouble; all they wanted was to get some supper. You see," continued the old man, with a chuckle, "they knowed mighty well I would shoot, an' I reckon they didn't want to be laid out jist then."

I said I didn't wish to expose them to any danger. Rather than that I would leave their house. But Old Yank remarked, sternly: "Sonny, you stay right here! I kin take keer of myself, an' you, too!"

Then he led me to a bed that seemed indeed luxurious after the night I had passed in the woods. Caucus made himself comfortable in the stable with the horses. He said he could " take to de woods quicker from de barn den de house."

_____

CHAPTER XV.

THROUGH THE GAPS.

THE next morning one of the girls came hurriedly in, and after a whispered conversation with her father, the old gentleman said : " It don't seem to be hospitable to tell you to git, but you light right out. My darter says she heerd from a passing nigger that a squad of Morgan's cavalry is coming along this road. Keep dead north 'till you strike the bend of Cane River ; then go northeast, and a little before you get to Flat Rock in Mitchell County you'll strike Tittle's place, what I told you about."

Under these circumstances, Caucus having brought the horses up, we started out at a pretty lively jog, though we could not make very fast time, for it was raining heavily and the road became very muddy. Meeting one or two people, of whom I inquired if there were any mules to be obtained about here, as I was getting them for the Confederate Government, we passed along, I saying I was in a hurry as I must get back to Raleigh in a little over a week.

During the day I spoke to the negro, telling him that he had better return to South Carolina with the horses, as, the country being mountainous, I would walk almost as fast as I could ride, and that the dangers ahead of us were very great.

" No, sah ! " returned Caucus, showing the whites of his eyes. " Dis chile neber goes back to Carolina. Dar's freedom ahead of him, and he's gwine to git dar, sure, dis time. Can't turn me back now, Massa Bryant, not eben wid a six-shooter ; I goes wid you ! "

And so he did for nearly two months without a word of complaint.

After traveling up hill and down dale for a couple of hours, we came to the bend of Cane River which Caucus had seen before ; then swinging off along a bridle-path,

that led to the northeast, after making several inquiries
of people who were armed and looked at us with suspicion, I found myself in view of my stopping place, and
to my surprise saw two Union soldiers standing in front
of the house. I was informed by Mrs. Tittle as I rode
up that her husband had gone to the mill for grist. She
seemed very embarrassed until I came up to her and
gave her the grip that Old Yank had shown me.

At this, apparently having lost all fear of me, she said
that these two soldiers had escaped from Salisbury
prison, and were making their way to the Union lines.

I suggested to these men that for their own safety they
had better immediately change their clothes for those of
ordinary citizens, and they, having a few greenbacks in
their pockets, managed to buy from the family enough to
clothe them.

Soon after this Mr. Tittle returned, and told us we had
better be on our way, as some cavalrymen were riding
about the country looking up deserters.

He said : " The best thing you can do is to go back,
because it will take sand in your gizzard and no weak
knees to tramp between here and Knoxville, for the
rebels around would just as soon shoot you as a chicken,
and the Unionists ain't no better."

I said : " I must go through ! "

" Very well ; but make up your mind it is better to get
out of the highways and go over the hills and mountains.
You'd better give up your horses."

I said that as long as I had a horse I would keep to
the highways.

" All right, then ; if you are bound on the job, you had
better go straight up to the north to Little Rock Creek,
leaving Bakersville to your left, for if you go near
Bakersville, you'll be nabbed, sure ! "

Thanking him for his advice and directions, Caucus and
I hurried along on our way, into a driving rain. This
storm, as we went along, became thicker and more blind-
ing. Caucus had left all his knowledge of the country
behind him long ago. After passing along several
bridle-paths that seemed to lead nowhere in particular,
and just missing descending into a little valley in which
we fortunately in time saw a squad of six mounted men,
doubtless Confederate scouts, who would have done us

no good, we turned up into some thick undergrowth, the boughs of which made an uncertain protection from the wind and the storm. Here we built a fire, and tried to dry our clothes. Then we got something to eat and lay down to sleep exhausted, downhearted, wet, and miserable.

The next morning I was awakened by the negro shaking himself like a dog, and slapping his arms about. It had become quite cold. The rain had changed into snow, of which there was a slight fall now upon the ground.

"By gosh! I mus' git somewhar, or I'll freeze to death," said Caucus. "The snow is mighty uncomfortable."

"Yes," I replied, "we must get somewhere, but I don't like to travel in this snow. It will enable us to be tracked."

However, getting on our horses, after taking a bite of breakfast, together with some hot coffee that we succeeded in making over our camp-fire, we pushed along. Two hours afterward we could see from an elevated portion of the road a clearing and some farm-houses. These we made for, because the storm had so increased it was now unendurable. Upon reaching one of the houses, we saw no one but women. They appeared to be somewhat frightened, and immediately asked if I was a soldier. I told them I was not now on a warlike mission; that they need not be uneasy. Other women now made their appearance, and one of them seemed to be in such distress that I made some remark to her about it.

"Distress?" she replied. "My heavens! don't you know they killed my husband the other day before my eyes!"

I turned away from her, unable to say anything to such grief. The others informed me that he had given information to some of the Union scouts about there by which a Confederate soldier who was home on a furlough from the army of Virginia had been captured. That for this a party of bushwhackers had taken him out of his wife's arms in the middle of the night, and shot him to death in front of the door.

In this place the storm compelled us to remain all that day and night.

Anxious to get away, however, Caucus and I saddled up early in the morning and again tried to force our way in the direction that Tittle had told us to take. The storm came up again, and for three days we wandered about this part of the country, twice camping in the open, and once sleeping in the house of a man who boasted to me that he had helped lay out in the last two weeks three or four Unionists. With this man I made a desperate attempt to bargain for mules "for the Confederate Government." He had two or three, but I need hardly say that my price was too low for him.

On the fourth day the storm cleared, the sun came out, and we turned our faces westward. We had come much further north than we had expected, having wandered out of our path and being almost on the borders of Watauga and Mitchell counties.

Passing through a little gap in the mountains, we came on a plain that was a kind of base to the mountain ranges near us that lay on either hand about two miles away. Here we passed a farm owned by a gentleman who was an officer in the Confederate army, and I pumped a man working on the place about the roads beyond. He had heard that some soldiers were in the neighborhood, but didn't exactly know where they were.

We went southward from this place, following a narrow road, from which the snow had nearly disappeared. With this I was delighted, because our tracks in it would always be a direction for any party who wished to follow us.

After half an hour's travel we came to a large open field, where, to my astonishment, I heard the firing of musketry.

Caucus whispered : "Reckon we'd better stop and take a squint at dat noise ! "

Dismounting and sheltering ourselves behind a rail fence, we were able to discover the location of two or three men by the flashes and smoke from their guns. Beyond them, and separated from them by a deep ravine, we saw one or two other men return the fire from a clump of laurel trees. By the uniform of those nearest to us I judged that they were Confederate cavalrymen. The others seemed to be dressed in blue.

I had hardly made this observation, when I heard a yell from Caucus. "Golly ! Dey's after us !" and looking down the road perceived five or six troopers coming along the tracks we had made in the melting snow. I might have paused, surrendered to them, and tried to have made out my case as being all right ; but somehow or other, knowing that they were my enemies, my presence of mind left me, and, followed by the negro, I remounted my horse and spurred on my way. This was probably the worst thing I could have done, for a volley from the Confederate cavalry overtook us, and killed my horse under me. Crying to Caucus to follow me, which he did, jumping from his horse for that purpose, I climbed over the rail fence, ran through the undergrowth and went down into the ravine, which I crossed to the other side.

Here I had a moment's breathing space, in which to regret my lack of presence of mind. Had I remained and faced the Confederate cavalry, I could probably have persuaded them that I was all right. Now, having fled from them, no such chance was open to me. I looked at our poor horses, one dead, and the other in the possession of the Confederates, and had the sorry satisfaction of knowing that, with the exception of the papers on my person, my two pistols, and the money in my pocket, all my worldly goods were in the hands of my pursuers. However, armed as we were, for I had given one of my six-shooters to the negro, I concluded that we could defend the ravine against any horsemen who should attempt to cross it. These thoughts had hardly passed through my mind, when I heard a voice near me, and turning round saw a man in blue uniform.

He said : " I reckon, you are on the same side of the gulch as we are, stranger. Come right along, and help us stand the cavalrymen off ! "

Caucus and I silently followed him. In the undergrowth were three other men, one of them in the uniform of a lieutenant in the Federal army. He was armed with a Henry rifle, and replying to the fire of three or four Confederate troopers, who were about a hundred and fifty yards off, on the other side of the ravine. The lieutenant, using his gun with great accuracy, kept the Confederates at bay, and injured one of them. One of his men, however, was wounded also. The Confederates drew off.

"Now, boys," he said, "we must get through to Steiner's as quickly as possible, before those chaps can get around. Follow me!"

Two of us assisted the wounded man, who had a ball through his leg and appeared to be in a good deal of pain, and we hurriedly put off by a mountain path, ascended quite a hill, and, after traveling about three miles, descended into a valley occupied by Steiner, a man celebrated in that region for his Union proclivities. The Confederates had had him out to hang him once or twice, to make him tell the hiding-place of Union refugees, but the old fellow was of such grit that they became ashamed of torturing him, and always let him go.

He was mending a wagon in his blacksmith's shop when we came up.

"Wal," said the old man, "you didn't git out this time, did you? You North Carolina Union boys, born right here, an' knowing every part of the way from here to Knoxville, couldn't get through Morgan's cavalry!"

"We will do it next time," said the lieutenant. "We have brought back a wounded man to leave him with you."

"All right; I'll take care of him; but who are these two strangers?"

"I am darned if I know, but I reckon they are on our side, and have got sand in them. They helped us stand off Morgan's cavalry. As for the nigger, he's a red-head, and that's a true sign of fight. This gentleman's his master, I reckon."

"Now," he said, turning to me, "I suppose you are bound the same way we are. I know every step of the road from here to Knoxville, and if you have lost your horses you had better join us, as five are better than two, to stand off any scouting parties. Your horses would not have done you much good from now on, as you would have to take to the mountains, for none of our side can travel the roads and live to get through."

I explained to the lieutenant and Steiner exactly my position, and how I came to be where he found me.

"Very well, Mr. Bryant," he said; "I can put you through if any man can. Is it a go?" and he offered me his hand.

In return, I gave him the grip Old Yank had shown me, and Steiner said : "That's the talk ! Now I knows you are square and right."

The party, however, was too worn out to travel that evening, and we all went to sleep with our pistols under our heads or by our sides, for Morgan's men might be upon us again before morning.

We were now in a very rough country. The Blue Ridge towered up range above range before us, and presented a grand spectacle, separated by gaps through which the water courses ran toward the Tennessee, pointing out to us the way to the Union lines through which many of these streams ultimately ran. The lieutenant knew every gap and water course in these mountains, and every inch of the country to Knoxville beyond them. This was fortunate for us, as Longstreet's scouts or foragers were all through this region, having been thrown out from his army now before Knoxville. The lieutenant had been detailed to go through this part of the country to gain all the information he could for the commanding officers of the Union troops in the valley of the Tennessee.

Though a cavalryman, he had taken this perilous journey on foot, as he could travel with even more celerity and less danger through these mountains in that manner than on horseback. He was active, fearless, and an untiring walker.

Our first tramp was about twelve miles, to the house of Mr. Middleton, a Union man. Here the lieutenant expected to meet two more men who were going to attempt to pass through the lines. The day was misty and foggy, and a little snow fell. At six o'clock in the afternoon we stopped at a house near the roadside, and had some hot coffee, made as usual in this region from chicory. About seven o'clock we started again in the rain, and two hours afterward moved down into a little valley about half a mile in width, the land being cultivated by two or three different farmers. The lieutenant told me that one of the farmers had a son in the Union army, while his neighbor had one in the Confederate, as was often the case in the border States.

After leaving this place about a mile and a half, we met two citizens on horseback. One of them asked us where we were bound. We told him most anywhere.

He replied. "You will meet with a great big hinderer that will bother you, if you don't mind."

"What is that?" asked the lieutenant.

"The Regulars."

"Who and what are Regulars?"

"Oh! they just go about and catch anybody they can lay their hands on. Sometimes they take a man out and shoot him; sometimes they hang him. A hundred yards from here we can show you a tree where they hung a man. Our advice is for you to watch out, or they will get you sartin."

With these words the two men rode off, but I noticed that the lieutenant had his pistol out and watched them. He told me he thought they might be the advance guard of the Regulars. He kept his eye on them, so that if they did attempt to fire on us as they rode away, he would have "the drop" on them. After we had gone on a few yards, the lieutenant said that we had better leave the roads at once and get up on the mountains. To this, knowing the desperate character of the so-called "Regulars," we all assented, and taking a very circuitous route through the roughest of ravines and over the highest and rockiest of hills, we arrived at Middleton's about eleven o'clock in the evening.

Middleton knew our lieutenant, and invited us into the house, which was on a little elevated ground at the fork of two roads. Here we found the two men who were going with us through to Knoxville. They lived in an adjoining county, and had been dodging about for several months to keep out of the Confederate army. This made our company seven men, with the lieutenant to guide us, in whom I soon began to have very great confidence.

The country about us, Mr. Middleton said, was alive with Confederate scouts and bushwhackers, and he recommended that we should not remain there that night. After consultation we decided to take his advice, and to get an old hunter, Zeke Carter, to pilot us across some twelve or fifteen miles to a road intercepting the one we had left. Zeke was an old bear hunter, and lived in a log hut about two miles up in the hills. Our host volunteered to guide us there, and resuming our walk, after crossing a stream, we reached Zeke's house. A faint light coming through the crevasses between the logs showed us he was at home.

Middleton hallooed, and Zeke came to the door. Then we agreed, after some haggling, to pay him twenty dollars for his services—a sum of money that made the old mountaineer's eyes twinkle. He was a hard-featured, stoop-shouldered, long, gray-bearded customer, with piercing black eyes. He invited us into his cabin, while he cooked the rations for his trip, which he told us would last, probably, three or four days.

Upon the walls of his domicile were deer-horns, and bear and coonskins, which told of the old fellow's success with his rifle in the mountains.

Leaving his house about midnight, he remarked : " Well, boys, we've got a good-sized hill to climb ! " and shouldering his old-fashioned rifle, told us to follow him, which we did, in single file. After a terrific tramp of about ten miles over rocks that cut my boots into pieces, and once getting lost from the party, and having a great deal of trouble to find them in the darkness, I, together with the rest, came to what Zeke said was a good place to camp.

This was uttered in low tones, to avoid attracting the notice of bushwhackers, for our route led into the " Sweet Water valley," which Zeke remarked was one of their breeding places.

We were nearly at the end of our journey for the night, when Zeke cried : " Halt, Gol darn you ! Halt ! "

" Well, what is it ? " came out of the darkness from a man a few paces in advance of us.

" Who are *you* ? " inquired Zeke.

" Well, we are scouting around, and, if you say so, we are friends."

" How many of you ? "

" Only two ! "

" Where are you going ? " asked the lieutenant, coming forward.

" Oh, we're going about, and I shouldn't wonder if you were like . us. Ain't you men going to the lines ? "

To this the lieutenant cautiously replied that we were taking in the country, but Zeke, who was of an impatient disposition, said, " By the etarnal ! there's no use fooling around here! You come with us, and we'll soon know you, or you will know us!"

As we were eight men and they were but two, hesitation on their part was out of the question. We treated them as prisoners, and soon marched them to the spot that old Zeke had picked out for our camp. This was a level spot of ground in horse-shoe shape, about fifty feet in diameter, standing against a rocky cliff, over which a stream of pure mountain water descended.

This place overlooked a little valley, between the Iron and Yellow mountains, and was much frequented by hunters and travelers, as it afforded such fine water. Upon examination, the two men we had overtaken proved themselves all right, and, appointing pickets to relieve each other, we lay down, worn out with nearly twenty-two hours' steady tramping. In fact, as Caucus remarked, as he snuggled up to the camp fire, " Dis road to freedom am a mighty hard one to trabel."

Too exhausted to sleep, I lay awake, for some time my thoughts turning back over the mountains to the south of me, trying to imagine how my wife had fared in the two weeks I had already been away from her.

When I awoke it was mid-day. As we prepared breakfast, I looked out over the ledge above which we were encamped, and seemed to see a thousand mountains in this Switzerland of America.

Our guide now told us that it was about seven miles over the hills to the place where he would leave us. These seven miles seemed an immense distance to me. My feet were sore, my shoes were coming to pieces. My appearance was that of a not over genteel tramp, as I had not shaved since leaving Spartanburg. However, I followed the party down the steep descents and up the high hills again, repeating the operation several times before we reached our stopping place.

In about half an hour's travel we came to a public road, which we were compelled to cross.

Coming from the direction of French Broad River in Tennessee, it ran into Mitchell County in North Carolina. Old Zeke instructed us to walk over this road backward, so that our tracks would mislead people as to the direction in which we were traveling.

After this piece of strategy nothing happened of

importance until we came in sight of an old clump of
trees, when old Zeke told us of a terrific combat he had
had with a bear, which had nearly whipped him.   In
fact, the old man's arms had not even now entirely
recovered from the hugs that Bruin had given them.

Passing a simple shanty occupied by a squatter, who
apparently was too old to fight, but of whose feelings and
sympathies there was no doubt, for he cursed us for
Union men as we tramped past, we paused to look at a
valley below, through which coursed the beautiful Doe
River.   It must have been eight or ten miles away, but
looked very lovely in the distance with the afternoon
sunlight upon it.   As we trudged up to the crest of the
hill, on leaving this spot, the lieutenant suddenly paused.

I thought he had noticed some of the enemy ahead,
but instead of that, he pointed to the west and said :
" *The first sight of Tennessee !* "

Looking toward the place he indicated, we could
see the Bald Mountain of the " Smoky Ridge " that
divided North Carolina from its more western neighbor.

While drinking in the view of this, to us, " Promised
Land," old Zeke said : " Wal, boys, I'm going to get
back to my shanty, but I'll shake a fist with you all, first.
Keep your eyes open and your powder dry !   That's what
you want.   Good-by ! "

With this the old frontiersman turned upon his tracks,
and striding down the path, was soon out of our sight.

It was now getting dark, and we determined after
dinner that we would start again on our way.   The route
was directly over the ridge of the mountains, and we had
but little difficulty in making the three miles, which
brought us to the house occupied by Mr. Cunningham, a
good Union man to whom we had been directed by the
guide.

Cunningham advised us to be very careful and not
travel by the road, as he had heard of several scouts or
Confederate cavalrymen being in the immediate neighborhood ; so after supper we concluded to go on at once
through the night.

Tempted, however, by the easy traveling on this highway, we disregarded Cunningham's advice and determined
to travel upon it, though it greatly increased our risk.   We
kept on close together, sending Caucus a hundred yards

ahead to act as scout, as we knew a negro would create less suspicion with Confederate soldiers than a white man.

We had hardly gone this way half an hour when Caucus came softly back to us and remarked : " Golly ! dar's voices ahead ob us."

The lieutenant went with him and reconnoitered ; but hearing nothing, we started on.

Hardly had we reached the top of the ridge and become outlined on the sky, when two or three shots whizzed past us from a clump of trees. We knew that we were ambushed, but could see nothing of our enemies, though another volley came in our direction. The night was dark, and, by the lieutenant's orders, we had thrown ourselves on the ground ; consequently none of us were hurt.

" Boys ! " said the lieutenant, " all of you shoot two or three barrels, and we will make them think there is a whole company here."

The banging of our pistols sounded like the regular file firing from a platoon.

" Another shot each, and then follow me ! "

We fired one more volley, which was returned, then followed the lieutenant, who left the road and started up the mountain. After a little, the lieutenant said : " Now boys, hurry to the gap, and get through to the other side of this range. It will be some five or six miles out of our way, but we must get there before those fellows ; otherwise we will have another fight for it."

He had been through this portion of the country before, and knew the roads almost by instinct ; so up hill and down hill we followed him with sore and weary feet.

This was especially so in my case. I had not been accustomed to traveling on foot, and kept up with great difficulty with the others, for my shoes, being worn out, filled with gravel and dirt at every step. But at last coming to a little running stream, we all sat down for a short rest, and I washed my feet in the cold water and wrapped them in cloth torn from the lining of my coat. This relieved them somewhat, and we again started on our journey. Nearing the gap about daybreak, to our consternation there were three or four lights right down in it.

9

"Camp-fires," said the lieutenant. "We can't get through there, and this is the only place we can cross without going around by Littleton's, three miles more. Shall we try it to-night, boys?"

The general verdict was against this, for we were in no condition for rapid traveling, and if discovered by a superior force, would be sure to be captured. So we turned out of the path, and, finding a place in a deep ravine, made a camp, though we dared not light any fire.

After drawing straws to see who should stand guard, all but the picket lay down, and I soon forgot that I was a refugee in the mountains of North Carolina.

It seemed to me that I had hardly slept a minute before the guard came and touched me on the shoulder. I woke with a start. Some Confederate troopers were riding along the road not two hundred yards from us. Fortunately they did not notice us, and about dusk next day we resumed our journey to the house of a family who lived in the gap, and were friends of our lieutenant.

They advised us not to remain, as the cavalry would undoubtedly return before long, and recommended us to go to Jim Boles' house, who would direct us on our way.

As we came near that gentleman's front fence, Mr. Boles came to the door, gun in hand, and shouted, "Who's thar?"

"Come out here, Jim, I want to see you!" said the lieutenant.

"Pshaw!" returned Boles. "That trick is played too often. What do you want, and who are you?"

"I am Lieutenant Hanson, of the Fifth Kentucky Union Cavalry, whom you well know."

"Oh, yes; I recognize your voice," replied Boles. "Come right in, and bring your crowd with you. It's lucky you applied to me, or you would have been in the Rebs' hands inside of an hour. There's a camp of 'em about three miles from here, and you have got to go around by Mix's place." This meant a walk of about fifteen extra miles.

Boles' two daughters, sixteen and eighteen, strong and healthy, volunteered to pilot us. Our lieutenant was not exactly sure of this part of the route. so he said, " All right, girls; I'll take you as guides, but you must let me pay for it ! "

" No, sifee, not a cent ! " they cried. " Let's go now ! "

" What, to-night ?   We are fearfully tired."

" If you don't go now, you won't go at all.   You'll be bagged sure in the daytime."

There was nothing for it, tired, worn out and hungry as we were, but to travel fifteen long and weary miles that night.   The girls said they would go in advance about thirty or forty yards, carrying a white handkerchief, and whenever they waved this, we were to halt and wait for instructions.

We made about three miles the first hour, without any interruption ; then saw two camp-fires, and the girls came back to us, and said we would have to go a little higher up the mountain in order to get through the gap without being discovered.   Notwithstanding we did this, we soon came so close to these fires that we got a very good view of the picket on his beat.   We saw a dozen tents, and beside them some soldiers cooking by the fire, and others playing cards.   A few hundred yards further on the girls stopped and waved their handkerchiefs, then returned, and said there were some men on the roadside by a fire partially burned out.

Taking us back a short distance, they ascended a little path that wound around the side of the mountains, very steep and difficult, but by which we soon passed the enemy who lay below us not three hundred feet.   The thick bushes and flinty rocks of the path tortured my sore and blistered feet, continually reminding me of what " Old Yank " had said to me,—that " Jordan was a hard road to travel."   Trudging along as well as I was able, at last we came to a bridge that crossed a mountain torrent.

Here the lieutenant said he would wager that more men had been shot and killed to the square foot in this section, than anywhere else in the United States.

To this pleasant assertion none of us replied.   We were probably weighing in our minds the individual pos-sibilities of our being added to the number.   After another tiresome climb, we crossed the ridge, and keep-ing straight down until daylight, arrived at the house of Mr. Mix, to whom our youthful and faithful guides pre-

sented us as guests for the day. Here we met two more
men who were seeking to avoid conscription in the rebel
army by making their way through the lines to Knoxville.

The whole party were too tired and exhausted to think
of traveling, and we concluded to lie over with this hospitable mountaineer for two days, and then, owing to the
sickness of one of our party, a West Virginian, an additional twenty-four hours.

CHAPTER XVI.

THROUGH THE LINES.

THIS delay was very welcome to me, as my feet were
in a fearful condition and my boots were falling off
them.

I divided my time at this stopping place between
sleeping and an attempt at the cobbler's trade, repairing
my footgear with the aid of Caucus, who was much more
expert at this work than I.

The two girls who had piloted us so devotedly over
the mountains remained here a few days, Mr. Mix
offering to take them home again in his wagon.

Every night we gathered around the big log fire in the
house, telling stories about our adventures during the
war. On one of these evenings I was astonished to
hear our lieutenant state that he had had a brother in
the Confederate army who was killed at Shiloh, while
leading his company against a Federal battery. But
it was thus throughout western North Carolina—family
was opposed to family, and brother was against brother.

On the third night of our rest at this place the lieutenant and Mr. Mix both became very anxious. They said
that we had remained so long here that the chances were
that some Confederate troop must pass soon ; consequently our guards must be constantly on the alert.

" You see," Hanson said, " if Schofield crowds Longstreet all his soldiers will be called in, and some will be
bound to pass here. Now, I'm pretty sure Schofield will
be crowding Longstreet about this time ! "

My turn for picket duty came at three in the morning. I was posted about a hundred yards from the house in which our men slept, dressed and armed. The moon was still bright, though rapidly descending to disappear behind the mountain tops.

I had watched perhaps an hour, when I heard a sound of horses' hoofs at a distance ; then, after listening a moment, the clank of sabers. I looked up the road, and in the full moonlight counted, perhaps half a mile away, twelve cavalrymen, riding leisurely toward the house.

In a minute more I had aroused my party. "We can fix them from behind that stone wall," muttered the lieutenant. "We're nine, they're only twelve. Follow me !" but as he gave this order his glance fell upon Mr. Mix's wife and children, and the two girls. Then he paused.

"Don't mind us !" muttered Mix between his set teeth.

"But I must,—think of your little ones, man. If we whipped those fellows at your house, when we'd gone they'd come back and take revenge upon you and yours. We don't repay hospitality that way."

"God bless you !" cried Mrs. Mix. "Go up that stream, and when the rebs go, I'll bring you all breakfast."

"Follow me, men, quick !" muttered our commander. "We'll retreat now, but we'll not retreat always !"

We silently followed him out of the rear of the house, and obeying Mrs. Mix's instructions, were concealed before the Confederates arrived. Shortly after daybreak one of the girls came out and found us. She said the rebs had gone on, and that Mrs. Mix would now bring us our breakfast. This she did in about half an hour. As soon as this was finished, the lieutenant ordered a start, and we bade our hospitable friends good-by. Though we tried again and again to make them accept something from us, for all they had done for us, this was refused, and the two beautiful girls even became indignant at our offered remuneration for their dangerous all-night tramp with us through the gap.

We were now in the western part of Mitchell County, and had next to cross through the valley lying between the Nolachucky River, and the dividing line between Tennessee and North Carolina. A portion of our route now lay along this stream which empties into the French Broad in the northern part of Cooke County, Tennessee, this being the most direct way to the Big Smoky or Bald Mountains.

Thus we traveled until about three o'clock. At one point, where the river takes a bend of nearly two miles, we forded it, and near the center found it some three feet deep. We had hardly got out and dressed, before two white men and a negro walked down a little path to the place where we had entered the stream. Our lieutenant called out and asked the men who they were, and what they came there for. One of them replied that they had seen us from a small log shanty at the top of the hill. They noticed that we were not soldiers, and consequently thought that we were refugees. They were of that class themselves, and said they had come back from the Nolachucky gap because they had found it guarded, and they could not get through, without going over the Bald Mountains, which were the highest and roughest in the State.

It was evident now that we either had to run the gauntlet of Confederate soldiers in this gap, or do some of the hardest work of our journey. The men who gave us this information refused to go on with us, as it was too dangerous.

Our lieutenant, however, said : " There's nothing like trying ! " and taking his advice, our whole party started along a road at which we had just arrived.

Its pleasant smoothness, so different to the flinty rocks of the hillsides, soothed our fears of immediate danger, and we concluded to try it for a mile or two, though it was a place from which, if we encountered superior numbers, there was no escape. The rushing river was on one side of the road, and a steep cliff upon the other.

We had hardly proceeded more than a mile, before the lieutenant, who marched a hundred yards ahead of us, came running back, and said : " Great Scott ! half a dozen troopers are coming down the road. We can't run ; we must stand 'em off, though I fear the noise of the firing 'll bring a crowd of them onto us! Every man of you behind a rock, and obey orders ! "

Caucus had already done this, getting into the stream, the bank of which and the trees on its border formed a

perfect ambush. "Come right heah, Massa Bryant!"
he cried, his teeth chattering with the ice-cold water that
had been melting snow the day before. Every rock had
its man. I had not a moment to lose, and jumped into
the river beside the negro as the squad of Confederates
turned the bend in the road.

Every one held his breath, they had nearly passed us
when, unfortunately, Caucus' teeth, stimulated by the icy
water, began to play like castanets, making a perceptible
noise.

"Gol darn it, what's that?" cried a Confederate
trooper and the squad paused to listen.

"Darn me if it ain't a rattlesnake out in winter," said
another, and he rode into the bushes on the bank of
the stream.

"Fire!" cried our lieutenant.

And a shot came from every rock about the surprised
soldiers.

The man who had turned into the bushes, yelled,
"Here's one of them!" and drawing his saber, jumped
his horse into the river to attack Caucus. At that
moment my revolver and the lieutenant's Henry rifle
spoke, and the man and horse floundered in the stream.
Wounded as he was, the trooper seized the negro, but
Caucus fought like a demon, using the butt of his revolver
as a club—apparently having forgotten to fire it.

But if the negro neglected the proper use of his weapon,
the others of our party did not ; and taken by surprise,
attacked apparently by a greater force, five soldiers
spurred for their lives down the road, while the body of
their comrade floated drowning in the stream beside
them.

"Quick, men!" yelled the lieutenant. "Out of here
like lightning! There'll be a hundred men scouring this
road in ten minutes!"

We needed no warning, but hurrying along after him
a few hundred yards, came to a place where the hills
were not so steep, and leaving the road, scrambled up
the precipice for some time ; then, crossing the ridge,
took refuge in a dense thicket of a second growth of
pine and fir trees that formed an excellent cover. Here,
placing a guard to prevent surprise, we lighted a fire,
beside which Caucus and I dried our clothes, while the

others cooked our meal, and determined upon our future movements.

The lieutenant now said that he should try the gap that night, going well up on the mountain side, to avoid the troops that occupied it.

" To-night ! " most of us groaned, for we were fearfully tired.

" Certainly ! to-night ! To-morrow the news of this fight 'll be there, and we'll have no chance of getting through—it is a close call even now ! "

We cooked a day's rations, as we would not be able to halt again till noon the next day, so our officer told us.

Then we struggled on after this indomitable fellow, Caucus grunting as he trudged by my side : " Dis am a reckliss country, 'pears to me, Massa Bryant, round heah. Dey'd jist as soon kill a nigger as a white man."

After a while the lieutenant ordered us to all stop talking. We were entering the gap through which the Nolachucky passes into Tennessee. Soon below us in the valley, as we tramped along the hillside, we could see camp-fire after camp-fire of the Confederate scouts guarding this notch in the mountain. We were not much alarmed at this, however, as cavalry could hardly follow us over the rocks in the darkness of the night, and our officer seemed to know every bypath of this part of the country.

Getting through this pass, near morning, the lieutenant informed us we were now in Tennessee.

" Praise de Lord ! de Promised Land ! " cried Caucus.

" Well, Cauk, you'll find it the cussedest, hardest Promised Land you ever struck. Look out, or they'll have you over Jordan ! " muttered our leader as he passed the word to march on.

We were leaving the Smoky range behind us. In a week or two our fate must be decided ; but as we descended the mountain into the valley of the Nolachucky, I could see light upon light, indicating more camps of soldiers, evidences that every step we advanced added to our danger of death, or capture. As day broke, we halted and went into camp in another secluded spot. Here we remained in hiding until darkness came on again to conceal us from Confederate patrols.

During the next two days we turned north to avoid the highway running toward Jonesborough, the country being mostly level, though we sometimes encountered a spur of the Bald Mountains. We were compelled to this roundabout course, as every high-road, cross-road and ferry was guarded by regular soldiers. Reaching Indian River, we were fearfully hungry, having had nothing to eat for over twenty-four hours. Seeing a house near by, I gave Caucus a dollar greenback and sent him to negotiate for provisions, as I thought a negro would create less suspicion than a white man.

The black being "fighting hungry," would have faced anything for a meal, and started off eagerly.

We watched the house and saw Caucus enter, the door being opened for him by a woman. After a few minutes he came out, traveling rapidly, but loaded with all kinds of eatables.

Five minutes after the woman came running out, apparently in the wildest excitement and rage, but Caucus had passed from her view.

When he came into camp the amount of provisions he had astounded me—a sack of flour, a side of bacon, two pans of biscuits, three dozen hard boiled eggs, a ham, and a lot of potatoes in a sack.

"All these for a dollar?" I gasped.

"Yes, sah!"

"What did the woman say?"

"She didn't say nothin', sah. She was in de cellar. I inviegled her into de cellar, and den negotiated de grub."

"Cauk, you'll be a forager in time!" laughed the lieutenant.

"I's larning, sah!" returned Caucus.

And so he did—a few months after this.

It was too risky to take back to the woman any portion of her provisions, and we were, perhaps, not over-scrupulous, for provisions meant strength, and strength meant safety; so we pushed along Horse Creek on the road toward Greenville.

Soon after this we came to a house, the owner of which was acquainted with our lieutenant. Here we expected to remain the night. It was just getting dusk as we halted some two hundred yards from the building, and the lieutenant went forward to see if it would be safe for us to show ourselves.

He soon gave us the signal to come on. At the doorway we were stopped by an old gentleman, who whispered that a Confederate soldier was inside upon a sick
bed, attended by his mother, who had arrived a few days
before from near Knoxville.

We were shown into a large room adjoining the one in
which the invalid lay. His mother came out and begged
us piteously not to disturb her almost dying boy, who was
down with typhoid fever. She said he wanted to see
some one of us. He guessed on what side we were, and
felt afraid for his safety.

The lieutenant nodded to me to go in, and I found the
young man very nervous, partly from sickness and partly
from anxiety. In a weak tone he asked me what we were
going to do, and whether we would molest him. Noting
his excitement, and seeing how it told upon him, I re-
quested him to give himself no uneasiness, for though
we were Union men, making for the front, we would
attack no one who did not disturb us. This seemed to
relieve him very much, and his mother followed me to
the door, and blessed and thanked me for having mercy
upon her boy.

Never was I so impressed until this moment with the
fearful passions of this time, that made a man, whom
every instinct of humanity would make us pity and assist,
fear we would kill him as he lay sick upon his bed.

The old gentleman invited us to remain for supper, but
told us if we stayed all night we had better sleep with our
boots on, as we would probably be gobbled up before
morning.

We took his advice, and his supper, and our host was
kind enough to pilot us to a spot between two hills where
we could make a fire without being observed from the
road.

Placing sentries, as usual, we passed the night unmolested. Early in the morning our friend came to us
and said he would get us some breakfast if we would
come down to the house.

Accepting his offer, while at table a little darkey came
in saying there were soldiers at the gate, and looking out,
I saw two men on horseback armed with rifles. Our
lieutenant, noting their number, called to them to come
in and join us.

They looked at us in surprise, but acquiesced, and after discovering who we were, one of them jocosely remarked that we had better watch out or they would take us prisoners.

"You will have a fine time of it, as we are heeled, and some one will be hurt!" returned Hanson.

One of them replied : "Just wait at this house for an hour, and we will change your mind."

The other told us not to mind him, as he was good at bluffing.

By this time we had come to the conclusion that these men were in advance of others ; consequently, while the two soldiers were still at breakfast, we started out at a quick pace on our journey, and went southward toward Cedar Creek, not following any road, but going through woods and fields, which would render pursuit by horsemen very difficult, the lieutenant telling us he knew a family living near Salem, about twelve miles distant, and if we could get there safely, we could learn enough about the position of the troops to aid us in determining our future movements.

To reach this place, however, we would have to travel through a thickly settled farming country southwest of Greenville. This could best be done at night, as we could detect the presence of soldiers by their camp fires. We camped in some timber till evening and then began our march. About eight o'clock in the evening we came to a house that stood near the fork of two roads. A woman appeared and asked who was there. We said we wanted to know if the way was clear to Salem. She replied that she was not quite sure. The day before she had seen soldiers coming from that direction.

Learning nothing definite, we passed on into the public road leading to the town, only disturbed by the barking of dogs, that had a habit of favoring us very often with their salutations at night.

At midnight we reached our destination. A woman opened the door for us. There was not a man on the place—every one of them being away in the army around Knoxville, except the woman's husband, who was hiding in the mountains.

She gave us a doleful account of things, and said she did not know how we were to get through, unless we

went north through the woods and approached Knoxville by a roundabout route.

This was out of the question ; it meant another two
weeks of refugeeing, and we were now almost too worn
out to travel.   Finally the woman advised us to go
northwesterly, direct toward Newmarket, and cross the
Nolachucky River above its junction with the French
Broad.   This was about ten miles, but we could reach it
by daylight, as the country was perfectly level and there
were no big streams to ford.

Acting on her advice, we set out.   We had hardly been
gone an hour before a rain-storm came up that made the
road very slippery.   We were rejoiced at this.   It would
tend to keep the Confederates under canvas.   Lights
appeared ahead of us, which we took for camp-fires, but
fortunately we did not have to go near them.

We reached our point in safety, and stopped about
half a mile beyond the junction of the two rivers in a
farm-house, where we found no one but a white man and
two negroes.   We asked the man to ferry us across the
stream.   He looked us over, then complied with our request, but in a very surly way.   The size of our party was
too large for opposition, and he took us over in two loads.

As he landed us he remarked that we would have a
nice time getting through the lines, and that he would
not like to be in our boots.

Thanking him for his trouble, we marched in the direction of Newmarket, intending to leave it on our right
and to pass southwest toward Strawberry Plains.   From
here on we were satisfied that we would meet in the roads
none but soldiers, and were continually on the alert.
It was now about eight o'clock in the morning, when
we came to a little creek and concluded to camp.   We
had traveled all that night, and most of the day before,
and nature compelled us to rest.   We halted at a little
log cabin back of a piece of woods three hundred yards
from the road.   It was quite secluded, and not apt to be
seen by people riding by.   No one came near during the
day.   We slept on the floor by turns—one of us always
being on guard.

During this time I patched up my shoes as well as
I could with strings, and tied them to my feet, from
which they had nearly fallen.

Often during the day we heard the noise of march-ing soldiers, but were fortunately too far from the road to be discovered. A battery of artillery also galloped past.

All this indicated some movement on Longstreet's part, but what we could not tell.

The lieutenant, however, said : " I think he has got to retreat. Judging by the number of men that are now coming in, he has called in most of his detached parties, but by to-morrow at this time we will probably know all about it."

" Why so ? " I asked.

" Because then we'll either be in the Federal lines, prisoners, or gone to glory ! "

" So soon ? "

" Certainly ! We can't keep dodging through the rebel army forever. If we stay here, we're bound to be caught in a day or two. Now, I've picked out our cross-ing-place on the Nolachucky—it's twelve miles from here. By a forced march, we'll get there before day breaks. If we get across alive, half an hour 'll place us in the Union lines. As soon as dark, we start to make the attempt."

If we were successful in getting through, our leader would go to his regiment and we would separate. Feel-ing that this gallant man's services deserved some recog-nition from us, I tore a leaf from my memorandum book and wrote :

" Whereas, we the undersigned, members of a party of Union men struggling to get away from the Southern Confederacy, have been guided with consummate tact, judgment, self-denial and bravery, by Lieutenant Hanson of the Fifth Kentucky Union Cavalry, we extend to him our sincere and heartfelt thanks, and, while we are unable to reward him substantially, we give to him our best wishes and best hopes that he may pass through this war safely, and when these troubles are over, may enjoy the rest of his life in health and happi-ness."

This being signed by us, I read it to the lieutenant, who said he would place that bit of paper in his bosom, preserve it from all harm, and always treasure it during the remainder of his life.

We now began our walk that would bring us to the crossing of the Nolachucky River, at a place ten or twelve miles from Knoxville. Along the road in the darkness we could observe evidences everywhere of the presence of soldiers. In some places fires illuminated the sky, while in others there were tent poles from which the canvas had been struck, and at one place we almost ran into a little camp of men on the side of the road. Avoiding this by a circuitous route through the fields, and coming out into the highway again, we had not gone far before we heard the galloping of horses. Leaving the road once more, because it was evident we were nearing the lights of almost a brigade of Confederates, and could not guess at what point we would run against its picket line, we kept on until two in the morning, when we reached our objective point near the river. A little house stood away from the road some fifty or sixty yards, and the Nolachucky was at least two hundred paces beyond it.

Across this river we could see lights, which were undoubtedly the camp-fires of some portion of Longstreet's army. The house was inhabited by a middle-aged woman and her daughters. There were no men near.

As we made known our purpose to get into the Federal lines, the lady said that the rebel picket line was across the river, where we could easily see the camp-fires. We then asked if we could cross the stream near there.

She said, " Not with any safety, as there were three men shot down there last night while trying to cross. They attempted to go just after dark. I warned them, but they said they would take their chances, and when I heard the musketry across the river, I knew they were gone."

We then asked if there was any other place to cross near there.

" Yes," she replied. " There's a bridge a little further up-stream, but that is guarded by a company of infantry, and I believe they have one or two guns there. There is going to be some movement. I can't tell what it is, because the troops have been traveling about here all day, and there has been a good deal of musketry firing in the front. I suppose there will probably be lively times to-morrow."

This made us most anxious to get into the Union lines. If Longstreet advanced, every foot he gained added another foot to the distance we had to travel, and took a way another chance of safety from us. We were now at the border line. Imprisonment and death were behind us. Death was, perhaps, before us.

We sat in the dark, early morning hours discussing the momentous question, whether we should attempt to cross or not. The woman knew the difficulty of the situation, and begged us for God's sake not to undertake the trip.

I told her we had been over a month on our journey, and we could not remain where we were in sight of the pickets; that boldness was our only chance. I then said: " Boys, I have come on this trip to go through the lines. We have come to the lines, and if I can get any one to go with me, I will get there ! "

I urged that the present moment, just before daybreak, was the best time to catch the pickets off their guard.

One man agreed to join me. The lieutenant hesitated, and said: " I do not think we can get across. I know you could not pass that picket line, with me in command of it, in the way you intend."

I replied: " Don't allow my rashness to influence you."

At that he jumped up and muttered: " I do not propose to allow any man to say I dare not follow him."

" Oh ! " cried the woman, " for God's sake, don't go ! If you do, you will never come out alive ! "

We thanked her for her interest, but there was nothing else for us,—we must go forward.

Only two of the men, with the lieutenant, would risk the crossing.

The others said it was too hazardous, they would wait developments.

As for Caucus, he didn't seem to think he had any voice in the matter, and as soon as I got up he followed me down to the woman's boat, which was an old and leaky affair, hardly useful for any military purpose, and as such neglected by the enemy. It was now between three and four o'clock in the morning. The whole party went to the bank with us. Unlocking the old batteau, we got in. Another man then decided to take the risk, and joined our party, leaving three who declined to go. We shook hands silently. It was now dangerous to speak, for the river was but a little over a hundred yards wide.

In order to make no noise, we used no oars, paddling

with our hands. To do this effectively I took off my coat, wearing a dark gray shirt underneath, that gave no light color to make me prominent in the darkness. This coat, which contained all my papers, I handed silently to Caucus, and he placed it on the thwart between us. Then we floated out into the stream.

CHAPTER XVII.

THE LETTER OF LIFE.

THE silence of the night was broken only by the rippling of the river against our boat, and the wash of its waters upon the bank we were rapidly nearing. The darkness of the night was only illuminated by two watch-fires that we dreaded. Steering to strike the bank midway between these fires, paddling with our hands for fear of disturbing the silence, we seemed to be totally unobserved. No noise was heard in the brush that lined the bank of the stream. No word came out of the silence of the forest, that was only separated from us now by a few yards of water.

I was now confident we would gain the bank, and probably half an hour would see us in the Union lines.

Suddenly from out the brushwood right in front of us came " Who goes there ? " from the hoarse voice of a Confederate picket.

The lieutenant who sat next to me whispered in my ear, " Overboard, for your life ! "

As he dropped over the gunwale, taking the side away from the bank, to obtain the protection of the boat from rifle-balls, I followed him, and diving under the bottom of the batteau, we floated silently down stream, just making exertion enough to keep ourselves afloat.

As I rose I heard the crashing fire of musketry and shrieks and groans from the companions I had left in the boat, and over all Caucus' voice, shrieking, " Fo' de Lord ! What to do now ? "

The lieutenant turned his head, and paddling close to me whispered : " Float down the stream before you try to make the bank. This musketry firing will rouse every

picket within a mile ; " then struck out strongly down the
river with the current.

I followed him, but he gradually passed out of my
sight into the darkness.

After floating down three or four hundred yards,
numbed by the coldness of the water, which had but a
short time ago left the snows of the North Carolina
mountains, I turned and paddled to the bank, drew myself up on the ground, and thought I had escaped, and
could now make my way to the Federal lines.

Numbed with the cold, I staggered into the bushes.
unfortunately striking a few twigs.

The next instant a couple of bayonets were thrust
against my breast, and I heard, " Surrender or die ! "

" I am your prisoner," I muttered, for, chilled with the
cold, neither resistance nor flight was possible.

" You are one of that boat's crew we fired into up the
river about five minutes ago ? " said one of my captors.

" Yes," I replied, for there was no good trying to deceive
them. " Who are you ? "

" Oh, we're some South Carolina boys, up here to
see that you Yanks in East Tennessee behave yourselves."

" Take him to regimental headquarters," said the sergeant of the guard, who had come up, attracted by our
noise.

I was searched, and then marched between a couple of
soldiers to a log house, about a quarter of a mile up the
river, which was the headquarters of the regiment—one
of Kershaw's brigade of South Carolina troops, a portion
of Longstreet's corps, which, after fighting in Virginia,
had come down with their commander into East Tennessee.

Their colonel was not here, being away looking after
the picket lines. The adjutant, who was at headquarters,
told me I would have to wait until that officer's return
before they would know what to do with me.

I asked his permission to stand in front of the fire to
warm myself, for my teeth were chattering so that I could
hardly speak.

" Yes," he said. " I suppose if we want to get any
information out of you, we have got to warm you up a
little ; but I reckon you will be warm enough—or cold

enough—before we have done with you. Judging from
your clothes, and the position in which you were taken,
you are a spy ! "

I said, " When the colonel comes I will explain to him."

" Very well."

So, the sentry keeping a close eye on me, though I
was almost too chilled to move, I warmed myself and
dried my clothes in front of the fire. It must have
been now four o'clock in the morning. A moment
after, the sentinel saluted an officer on horseback, who
galloped up, followed by an orderly. He dismounted and
passed in, giving me a hurried glance, and after a few
moments' conversation with the adjutant, said, " Any
papers found on him ? "

" No, sir."

" Very well. Let the prisoner be brought in."

I was accordingly marched into the log cabin, which
was made comfortable on the inside by a fire and a rough
straw mattress in a corner, with some blankets on it. A
coarse deal table, some writing materials, and two rough
chairs were the rest of its furniture.

As I entered, the officer gave a start, looked at me
sharply, then turning to the adjutant, hurriedly gave him
some orders, which sent that officer upon some duty away
from regimental headquarters. Next he directed the
guard to leave me with him, but to keep a strict watch
outside to see that no one came in while he talked
to me.

The door had hardly closed when he turned to me and
said, with rather a hoarse laugh, " By the Lord ! this is
an unexpected pleasure, Mr. Bryant. When did you
come from the earthworks on Morris Island ? "

With a start I looked at him, and as the voice came to
me, I recognized my old friend and whilom chum Harry
Walton of Columbia. The full beard he wore and the
bronzed complexion that active service had given him
had so changed him that for a moment I had not recognized him.

" Major Walton," said I——

" Colonel," interrupted he. " Death has promoted me
since I saw you last. Promotion in that way is pretty
rapid around here."

" Colonel Walton," continued I, " I know from what

you have said that you are aware that I was imprisoned on Morris Island."

" Yes, for desertion, I believe," he said. " Where is your passport ? "

" I have none ! "

" No passport, and coming through our lines in citizen's clothes ! How did you leave the earthworks on Morris Island ? "

" I was removed from them."

" Where to ? "

" To work on the fortifications on Stono River."

" When were you discharged ? "

" I have never been discharged."

" The second time a deserter ! Looks very bad for you, Mr. Bryant. In fact, fatally bad," he remarked, lighting a pipe and sitting down. " I presume I could shoot you after a drumhead court-martial here, without violating military etiquette. Probably I shall have to, if we are driven away from here to-morrow morning, as I expect to be."

I replied : " My life is in your hands, Colonel Walton, but I hardly think it noble to take—when he cannot defend himself—a revenge upon your old friend and college chum, because he was more fortunate than you in winning Laura Peyton's——"

" Stop ! " cried the colonel. " Don't you say that word. Don't you dare to say she loves you ! I will not believe it ! If she had loved you, neither you nor any man on earth could ever have left her. However, I shall do my duty. I shall take no revenge upon you. I will send you, under guard, to Chattanooga. A drumhead court-martial can dispose of you as well as I can, and no man shall be able to say that Harry Walton treated him ungenerously. I will do my duty, sir ! "

He called the guard, and was about to consign me to them, when an orderly, coming up, said : " Colonel, here's a nigger who insists on seeing you. He has heard your name, and will not be put off. I think he has some information for you."

As he said this, the red head of Caucus entered the circle illuminated by the camp-fire. The black was dripping from the river, but carried in his hand, apparently unwet, my coat that contained all my papers.

At sight of this garment, I knew that my last chance was gone. Before any court-martial where I was known by my true name, the passport for Mr. Bassett would convict me.

" 'Clare to goodness, I's real glad to see you, Colonel Walton ! " said the negro, with an attempted wriggle of delight. " Who would spect to drop on a South Carolina friend in dis part ob de country ? Does my eyes good, Colonel Walton, to see you, sah. All de time comin' up heah, I said, ' When will we come to Colonel Walton ? ' "

" Caucus," cried the colonel, with a laugh. " You are happier to meet me than your master. Take him away, and give him something to eat. Niggers are always hungry. But see that he doesn't escape into the Union lines, for his evidence may come up before us."

" Now you is talkin', colonel," muttered Caucus. " You kill three or four of us, and was a leetle rough on us at fus'; but you take good care of what is left ob us."

" Take him away," repeated Walton, with a wave of his hand, as if anxious to get the darkey out of his sight.

" Yes, sah ; I'm a goin', sah. I'm always ready to eat, sah ; but, Massa Bryant, I don't want you to tink I didn't take good care ob your clothes. Heah's your documents in 'em, dry as a bone. Your pass is all safe, sah," and to my horror, he placed the papers carefully on the table.

At the word " documents " the colonel paused a minute, and said, as Caucus was being led away : " I will examine these. Let the prisoner wait here until I give further orders. You can close the door, orderly."

Then, without any ceremony, he ran through most of the papers hurriedly, with an occasional exclamation of satisfaction, and looking at me, said : " I think your case will give a court-martial very little trouble. I do not care particularly to conceal my feeling regarding you. If you were shot to death twenty times, it would not cause you the misery that you have caused me."

" Colonel Walton," replied I, " the misery I caused you was not intended. We both loved the same woman. If I won her, that was my luck."

" Won her ? " he cried ; " why, she is too true a southern girl to ever think of you now. *Won her?* You have

won nothing but what a court-martial will give you!"
Then he went on looking over the papers.

After a few moments, a short, suppressed cry, as of a
man in mortal agony, came from him. Gazing at him, I
saw that the paper he looked at was the one letter I
had received from my wife.

With a pale face, apparently controlling himself by an
almost superhuman exertion, he strode up to me, and
whispered in a low voice : " Is this letter true ? Is—
Laura—Peyton—your—wife ? "

" Yes," I replied, " my beloved wife ! "

" Good God ! "

A moment after he forced himself to calmness again,
and, looking at the letter, muttered : " Yes, it is in her
handwriting ! " and read it through once more.

Then, apparently forgetful of my presence, he clasped
his hands to his face, sank down into a chair, and I could
tell by his short, quick breathing that he was fighting the
fight that all men have to make who love truly and lose
—a struggle against the despair of knowing that the
woman of your heart has gone from you forever.

" Colonel Walton," said I, " do you want me any
longer ? "

" No ! Tell the guard——"

I had moved to the door.

" Yes ! Remain ! "

I paused. He was staring at me with bloodshot
eyes. Then he burst forth : " My God ! she *did* love
you ! "

" Yes ! she loves me still ! " I cried, proudly.

" I know it ! Don't tell me about it ! From her letter
I can see she loves you. My God ! What am I to do ? I
cannot do my duty. If I do, I make her——"

And for over half an hour he paced the floor of the
cabin, sometimes wringing his hands, sometimes pressing
them to his head. After a time he became calmer, and
sinking into a chair, perhaps exhausted by the violence
of his passion, said to me : " Mr. Bryant, I will not disguise from you, when I saw you here, when I knew that
you would be convicted, and probably sentenced to death
as a deserter or a spy, that it made me happy. This
letter from the woman we *both* love tells me she is your
wife, and loves you as such. I had intended to send you

to Bragg's headquarters to be tried for desertion. What
mercy you would get you can guess, for Bragg is a man
who has no mercy on his own men—what mercy would
he have upon you, a northern one ? Your chances for life
would not be worth the snap of my finger. If I did my
duty, I should do this, and make the little girl I have
known and loved, who was my playmate when a child, whom
I love now, God help me, as a woman !—a widow. I would
break Laura Peyton's—I mean Laura Bryant's—heart !
My duty says one thing, my love for your wife another.
If I thought she did not love you, I could do my duty;
but this letter shows me that every beat of her heart is
yours. I cannot do my *exact* duty. I will compromise
with my conscience. Now in order to compromise with
my conscience, Mr. Bryant, you must do what I suggest.
It is your only chance of life. My regiment and I are
put here as a kind of sop to the Yankee maw, that will
swallow us, probably, to-morrow. This regiment is to be
sacrificed to save the division. It has been done often
enough on both sides before, during the war, and it is
going to be done now. I and my men know this as well
as the division general who orders it. We are to hold
the little bridge and this bank of the river "to the last
man "—that is my order—or until I receive a signal
from the hill back of us that two batteries are in position there that will check the Federal advance. By
that time the division will have passed along the road,
and the river cannot be crossed in time to do it any
damage. Now I am to defend this bridge to the last.
I will leave you here. There will be a great many
balls and shells falling about you, but I hope you will
get accustomed to them, as I am. I shall hold the
bridge to the last man. Do you remain here, and if
my men forget you in the hurry of the battle, don't
remind them; don't make yourself *prominent.* Pick out a
safe place. I want to save the husband of Laura Peyton,
the man Laura Peyton loves. As for me, I am glad I
have got this kind of work to do this morning. I hope
my bullet may find me. It will, some time ; and I can
give my life for the South with a better heart than I
could have, before I met you to-night."

CHAPTER XVIII

THE FIGHT FOR THE BRIDGE.

THE colonel staggered out.

As he did so, the faint light of breaking day came in through the open door of the cabin. Looking from a square hole in the log wall that served for a window, I was soon able to perceive the immediate surroundings of the place.

Just back of it flowed the river, crossed at this point a very little to the right of the cabin by a country bridge hardly wide enough to permit the crossing of an ordinary wagon. The structure of this was of the usual western kind, the girders and trusses being made of squared logs bolted together, and its planking consisting of two-inch rough lumber. The width of the stream, which was here deep and rapid, was but a little over fifty yards; consequently a single pier in the center of the river, made of a crib of heavy logs filled in with broken stone, was sufficient to support this bridge, which was in the form of two spans resting upon abutments on either bank and the single pier in the center of the current. Upon the opposite side of the river two field-pieces were stationed, and a rough breastwork of logs had been constructed to protect an infantry support. This at present was simply guarded by a sergeant and a few men, though the gunners were sleeping ready for action alongside the section of their battery.

Along the opposite bank of the river ran a country road, sometimes beside the water and at other times running off from it from a few yards' distance to fifty and perhaps seventy-five. This was only protected here and there by clumps of timber, and the march of a column over it with the banks on my side of the stream occupied in force by the enemy would be certainly disastrous and almost a military impossibility. After passing the bridge, however, a hundred yards or so, this road turned from the river into the country, which was hilly, and perhaps half a mile away there was a position from which a few batteries of artillery properly supported by infantry could check an advancing army.

Along this road from down the river were coming hurriedly, but apparently in good order and without confusion, the baggage-wagons of a division; the heavy muffled rattle of musketry could be heard down the stream some miles away, an occasional salvo of artillery mingling with and punctuating the roar.

It was evident that the Confederates were withdrawing from their position—one of the most difficult and dangerous operations in war when conducted in the face of an active and enterprising enemy. Like most military movements, its success depended almost entirely upon time. If attacked while moving along this road by the river, in case the enemy gained the opposite bank from which to enfilade its column with musketry and artillery, the result would be a fearful disaster. If the Confederates could gain unassaulted the position in the hills away from the river, they might bid defiance to pursuit.

In order to avoid any chances of losing the opposite bank of the river, Walton and his South Carolina regiment had been stationed there to hold it, even in the face of an opposing division of Federals.

But to move a large body of men takes considerable time, even when unassailed. The baggage-wagons had just begun to pass me; it would be near mid-day before the infantry and artillery of the division could be all withdrawn, and, by the noise down the river, the enemy were attacking now; Walton and his regiment must be sacrificed to military necessity. Even as I thought this, a dusty aide-de-camp came dashing over the bridge.

As I looked at this structure, any wonder in my mind that Walton was not reinforced vanished from it. The bridge was so small and narrow that a larger body of men than a regiment would have found it impossible to retreat across it, closely pressed by an enemy.

Walton was standing outside the cabin; the aide-de-camp rode up, and after a few hurried whispers, the colonel burst forth: " Then he refuses reinforcements, but I am to hold this position! "

" Yes! till you get that signal! "

" How long will that take? "

" Three or four hours! "

" Good Lord! There won't be many left of us! " muttered the colonel, gazing sadly at his men already falling in. Veterans of three campaigns in Virginia, and Antietam, Gettysburg and Chickamauga besides, his men guessed their fate also ; for I heard one of them remark to a comrade under his voice, as they passed the cabin, " Thar'll be a pretty general turning up of toes to-day, I reckon, Tim ! "

And the other, a boy of about nineteen, said : " Trouble you for a plug of tobacco. I'll take a last smoke for old Virginie ! "

Others, however, stood with compressed lips that grew pale as they thought of far-off homes they scarcely hoped to see again.

But in all this there was no murmur from any of them, and when the colonel ordered them to the front, they only answered with a yell and double-quicked to their line of battle.

All this time the roar of musketry down the river grew louder and louder, and dropping shots began to fall about the picket line of the regiment ; a few wounded men came crawling and limping from the front, for all this day I never saw any one assisted off the field by comrades—their numbers were so few, their need of men so desperate.

" They attacked you down the river an hour ago in force ? " questioned the colonel of the aide-de-camp.

" Yes, sir ! "

" Then there'll be a brigade in front of me in an hour, and a division before this is over. Report that I'll hold this bridge to the last man ! "

" Yes, colonel," and the aide-de-camp galloped off.

Calling to his adjutant, Walton hurriedly wrote an order, and said : " Let duplicates in writing be given to every line and staff officer of the regiment ; also to the first sergeant of every company."

" To so many ? " asked the adjutant, coolly scribbling on a wooden bench, though the rifle balls were finding their way through the trees and wounding men about us.

" Yes," replied the colonel. " By the time the signal for retreat is given, a first sergeant may be the ranking officer of the regiment, and I don't want to take any chances of sacrificing one more man than necessary."

Then he gave a sigh and went to the front, leaving his horse in charge of an orderly.

The position for the regiment to defend was rather favorable.

A small ridge, running nearly parallel to the river, and going down close to its bank half a mile below us, was about three hundred yards from me. This was heavily timbered, the trees running a little over the ridge from the river; while beyond them were open fields, over which the Federals must advance. Along the edges of this timber, at intervals, breastworks of logs had been hastily erected, each of these large enough to give shelter to a company front in skirmish line. Between these sharpshooters were placed in rifle pits, keeping communication open.

This line of defense was a very long one for such a small number of men to hold ; for I noted that the Carolinians were hardly three hundred, for at that time death had made many a regiment in the Confederate army look like a company.

But the roar of musketry down the river was approaching. I gazed behind me. On the right, across the stream, the last of the baggage-wagons was passing, and a regiment of infantry, already withdrawn from the line of battle down the river, was marching to take position in the hills up the road. Behind them I could see other regiments of infantry, and a battery of artillery.

The roar of battle came nearer, and now, from dropping shots in the front of the regiment the firing increased to volleys. This was steadily returned by the South Carolinians. A quarter of an hour of this, and from the noise in front of me a Federal battery had evidently got into position, for rifle shells fell into the timber about me, some of them striking the opposite side of the river, and one of them exploding in the marching Confederate regiment on the road, killing and wounding some of them. Five minutes after, another Union battery came into position. It was easy to distinguish this from the first, because its rifled guns fired peculiar shells, that produced unearthly noises and shrieks that seemed to come from almost a human voice.

As one of these yelling things went over the cabin I was looking from, the front door was hurriedly thrown open, and Caucus came running in, his red hair almost standing.

I cried, " Caucus, I am glad you have escaped so far."

" Yes, but I won't last long. I'se most gwine now— heah em ! heah em ! Oh Lord, deliber us ! " and as another shell shrieked over us, he groveled in a corner.

" You're not frightened ? " I asked, astonished, for the black had so often shown his courage.

" Yas, I's dead scared now ! I could stan' de bullets, and de bustin' things, but when I sees dat talkin' shell a twistin' an' windin' about in de trees, an' sayin', ' Whar's you ? *whar's you ?* WHA-A-AR'S YOU ? ' I can't stan' it no longer. One uv 'em chased me nigh onto five minutes afore I dodged in heah, an' den 'cluded he would take some ob de fellers on de other side ob de ribber. I was too good a dodger. Great Scotty ! Dar's anodder ! "

This last with an additional shudder as another shriek-ing thing knocked part of the roof off over our heads.

The Federals had evidently caught sight of our log-cabin, and judging it to be the headquarters of the regi-ment, were getting the range of it rapidly. Telling Caucus of this danger, I beckoned him to come with me, for the noise had now become deafening, and we could hardly hear each other speak. Unheeded by the Con-federates, who were too much occupied in the front, we took refuge behind the abutment of the bridge on our side the river, and underneath its planking. Over our heads we now could hear the groans and curses of the wounded, who limped and staggered, coming in from the front and crossing the bridge. The number of these indicated enormous losses, and was constantly in-creasing, while the fire from the front showed that not only a brigade but almost a division was engaging this one Confederate regiment. This fusillade now came also very heavily from either flank, both up and down the river, enfilading the breastworks and rendering them of little protection to the few men who were now so des-perately holding them ; falling wounded and dying by scores without any of the cheers, hurrahs and dashing excitement of a charge—only just staying there and hopelessly dying as a plain, commonplace, everyday duty —the hardest way to die.

This idea seemed to impress the black, for he muttered, looking at the thinning line of battle : " Golly, dose rebs dies jist as if dey was use to it ! "

The fight had lasted now nearly two hours. A couple
of batteries and the bulk of the Confederate division were
going past on the road across the river. The captains
of both these batteries held them, and I could see
them violently expostulate with their chief of artillery.
Apparently their expostulations were listened to. One
of the batteries immediately took position upon our right
flank across the river, in a field some two hundred yards
up the stream, opening a direct fire with its rifle-guns,
sweeping away little by little the line of blue that was
trying to edge behind and cut off the retreat of the
Carolinians. This reduced considerably the fire of the
Federal troops from that point. The other battery took
position immediately behind the road on a little eminence.
Spreading its six brass Napoleon smooth-bores (just the
arms for the purpose) in the form of a fan, and using
them at very high elevations as mortars, with reduced
powder charges, it succeeded in dropping its shells over
the Confederate line of battle immediately in the Federal
advancing column now forming for a charge. The
accurate service of these guns was very important ; to give
the proper range, an exact charge of powder was necessary.

The captain of artillery, leaving his battery, galloped
coolly across the bridge, through the hail of musket balls,
to the front of the Carolinians. I could see him talking
with Walton for a few minutes, watching where his shells
fell, and signaling to the orderly whom he had stationed
midway on the bridge to repeat his signs to the officer
in command of his battery. These evidently indicated
the amount of powder to be used, for this was changed
several times, until the range of the battery became very
accurate, for I could see through the trees shell after
shell exploding in the blue ranks that were moving
across the open field.

Having got his range, the captain of artillery galloped back across the bridge very coolly, though I noticed
he wiped some blood from a flesh wound in his shoulder
as he passed me. The roar of guns down the stream also
indicated that another battery had taken position, and was
protecting the left flank of the Confederate regiment ;
otherwise it could hardly have held its ground as long as
it did, for the line of blue was charging ! The slender

line of gray infantry waited till the blue columns got
within a hundred yards of its breastworks ; then it gave
forth its fire rapidly and continuously—so rapidly for the
number of men involved, that I knew they must have
collected and loaded the muskets of their fallen comrades
in order to obtain the great weight of fire. Under this
and the bursting shells from the Napoleon guns across
the river, the Federal line wavered and went back, leaving the yellow fields it crossed covered with spots and
splashes of blue.

Meantime the steady tramp of the infantry of the Confederate division, some of it going at double-quick, came
from the road behind me. Its last few regiments were
passing us, and the battery down the river was withdrawn
to go in position on the hills beyond. The work of the
South Carolinians was nearly over, but hardly one man
in three remained in this line of battle. The Federals
were again massing a brigade to charge it.

Four times in the last hour had Walton come back to
ask the lookout on the bridge if they had not seen the
signal from the hills in the rear. Two of the four non-
commissioned officers placed at that duty were wounded.
The third, a corporal, in command, always replied : " No,
colonel ! " and shook his head.

The last time Walton came, he limped a little from a
slight wound in the leg.

" Please mount your horse, colonel," begged the corporal.

" No, I can do better on foot yet. My God ! will
that signal never come ? I don't want all my men to die,
and this charge will settle us ! " and Walton, shading
his eyes with his hand, strained them to see if he could
catch the signal.

" It must be there ! " he muttered, then suddenly cried :
" *It has come !* "

And looking through the smoke of battle to the hills
beyond, I could discern the flags.

The colonel, wounded as he was, ran back to the line
of battle The necessary orders were given very quickly,
for the companies came in at the double-quick pursued by
a hailstorm of Federal bullets. But where was the regiment of the morning ? Each company seemed but a
skeleton squad, and half of these men were staggering

or reeling from wounds and loss of blood. Drawing in
upon their center rapidly, which still held its ground,
they lined the breastwork immediately in front of us,
and as the Federal charge came on, gave them one
crashing volley, while the Confederate battery behind us
dropped six more shells into the charging lines.

The blue was checked for a moment, and in that
moment Walton, with the ease of a veteran, withdrew
his men across the bridge.

While he was doing so, Caucus called my attention to
some occurences that were making his hair stand on end.

The captain of artillery, aided by a couple of pioneers,
had rapidly dug a hole in the center pier of the bridge.
Into this four men, running down, placed four kegs of gun-
powder. Walton turned from his men, and he and the
artillery officer both stayed and to this mine deliberately
attached a fuse. Then they coolly waited until the rear
guard had crossed the bridge, and reached the little
breastwork on the other side of the river. Before this
was done there was another heavy volley, and several of
the men sank dying as they crossed the stream, while
Walton himself gave a start that indicated he had received another wound, and the captain of the battery fell
down upon the bridge. Coolly striking no less than three
matches to get a light, under this fusillade that became
more deadly every moment, Walton deliberately lit the
port fire that led to the mine; then shouldering the
wounded artillery officer, staggered across and took position behind the breastwork to check the Federal advance
for the last time. Both the batteries of artillery limbered
up and galloped off after the Confederate infantry. A
division had been saved—a regiment almost annihilated.

But all this meant little to Caucus and myself now—we
looked only at the smoking fuse that would explode the
bridge under which we were concealed. The black's face
had become ashen. His chattering teeth said : "Golly,
when dis blows up, we blows up too !" The cross-fire
from the Federals and Confederates made it almost
certain death to venture on the bridge. Caucus, before I
knew what he was doing, plunged into the stream, and in
twenty or thirty vigorous strokes reached the center pier.
Up this he climbed, for it was not more than five feet
high, and, sheltered by the heavy log cribbing from the

Confederate musketry, deliberately pulled out the lighted fuse from the mine. For a moment the South Carolinians did not notice it, but a second after a cry from Walton came across the river. Cursing the black, he called to his men to follow him, and firing his revolver at Caucus, ran across the bridge.

The Confederates rose up, but the fire from the approaching Federals was too heavy. A few of them fell wounded ; the rest dropped again behind the breastwork.

A dozen strides brought Walton to the center of the bridge. He pulled out another fuse, and attached it to the powder, this time cutting it off very short.

His revolver firing had driven Caucus into the river, who swam back to me.

As the colonel was about to light the fuse, he paused, staggered, clapped his hand to his side, reeled and sank upon the bridge, the lighted port fire from his hand falling sizzing into the river. The Federal advance was already at our end of the bridge.

With a yell of rage for their fallen commander, the Carolinians rushed from their breastwork, charged across the bridge, and at the center the blue and the gray met. Clubbed muskets, bayonets, and even fists were used in the struggle.

Swept back by overwhelming numbers across the bridge, the Confederates bore with them the dead body of their officer—another hero fallen for that lost cause whose banner had already began to droop and whose stars began to fade.

As I gazed at this a wave of blue surged round me. I had not come to the Federal lines—the Federal lines had come to me.

CHAPTER XIX.

WHERE WAS SHE?

BEING in the Union lines did not seem to improve the position of either Caucus or myself. We were seized as Confederate prisoners.

I tried to explain to the colonel in command, but he

said : "I have no time to listen to you. Say what you have to say at brigade headquarters." Then we were started to the rear in a hurry.

This seemed to astonish Caucus very much. He sidled up to me, for we were huddled together with a few Confederate prisoners and stragglers that had been gleaned by the Federal troops, and muttered disconsolately :

" Massa Bryant, why is we always took prisoners ? Don't seem to make much diff'rence what side we gits on, we's took prisoners anyway ! "

" Move along there, and keep your wet rags to yourself ! " cried one of the guards sharply, as Caucus brushed against him with his dripping garments.

At this the negro looked at him and remarked, plaintively : " Dey always said in South Ca'lina dat if I come Norf I'd be treated almighty bad, an' seems to me dey was 'bout right. Here I is, come all dis way to freedom and darned if you don't treat me worse dan de Rebs. I was tole you would 'sider me as a brudder," and looking innocently at the man, he set his comrades into shrieks of laughter by saying : " Be'ant you an Abolitioner ? "

" No, you miserable coon—I'm a Democrat ! " very savagely cried the man who was, by his uniform, from one of the Tennessee Union regiments. " And darn you, if you don't shut up, I'll blow the top of your sorrel head off ! "

The look of unutterable astonishment and reproach with which Caucus gazed upon this unsympathetic boy in blue as he tramped along to the rear after this was pitiable in the extreme.

During this walk I meditated that the only way that I could be set right immediately was the chance that Lieutenant Hanson might have escaped. I questioned Caucus as to the fate of our companions. He said two of them had been killed and one wounded by the Confederate pickets. By throwing himself in the bottom of the boat, he had escaped without a scratch.

Upon my arrival at the rear I was sent first to brigade and then to division headquarters, the general of which, as the firing had already died away from the front, had time to attend to me. I told him I had just come from the battle.

" Battle ! " echoed he, with a smile. " Guess you

haven't been round the army much. That was only a reconnoissance in force."

I inquired of him if Lieutenant Hanson of the 5th Kentucky Cavalry had joined his command.

After some inquiries among members of the staff, he told me that he had. The lieutenant was sent for, and in a very few moments his explanations placed me and Caucus upon the free list.

Upon giving a detailed account of my adventures to the Federal commander, he very kindly furnished transportation for Caucus and myself to the North. Two days after this we were in Nashville, and two more took us to my home in Illinois. Here I had a small farm, which, during my absence in the South, it being but twenty miles from Chicago, had greatly increased in value. At the local post-office I inquired anxiously for letters for me. I had instructed my wife carefully as to how she should address and send letters to me by blockade-runners. I had been two months on the journey, which would have given ample time for a letter *via* Nassau to reach me; but there was none there.

I immediately wrote to Laura *via* Bermuda, and waited anxiously for six weeks, but received no reply.

It was now April of 1864. The blockade-runners were often captured or sunk; the letter service in the Confederacy was very uncertain. My epistle might have miscarried.

Despite the entreaties of my friends in Illinois that I would stay with them longer, I determined to go to Nassau, for my anxiety with regard to Laura had become unendurable.

Taking Caucus, who now seemed to think me bound to support him for the remainder of his life, and obtaining money for the purpose by borrowing a small sum upon my farm, I set out for Nassau.

Arriving there two weeks after my departure from Illinois, I forwarded another letter that six weeks after I knew must have reached the Confederacy, because the blockade-runner came back in safety. I had given the letter personally to the captain, who informed me that he had placed it in the post-office at Wilmington, North Carolina.

Again I waited anxiously a month. Still no letter.

During this time my excitement, agitation and misery became greater and greater. I did not dare to visit the Confederacy—certain death awaited me there ; yet I could hear no news of my wife. My next attempt I made in another way. I wrote letters to Judge Peyton, Miss Belle, and Laura's brother, as well as another epistle to my wife, and one to my friend Stuart Bee, and waited another month with no more satisfactory result.

All this time I had tried to make the acquaintance of passengers on the blockade-runners coming from South Carolina, but the only thing I could learn from them was that they thought the Peytons were all alive, but there was some sickness in the family.

At this information, I began to fear that my wife might have expended the small stock of money I had left with her on her sick relatives. I knew her unselfish disposition. I bought a draft on a local bank at Columbia, and forwarded it enclosed in another letter to my darling Laura.

It was now nearly August. At times I wildly thought of disguising myself and attempting to enter the Confederacy. I think I should have done something of the kind, for my desire to hear of my wife had now almost become a mania which was undermining my health, taking away my spirits, and shattering my nervous system, had not I about this time received a letter from Stuart Bee which ran as follows :

SAVANNAH, GA., *Aug.* 1, 1864.

MY DEAR BRYANT : Your letter containing the account of your marriage with Miss Peyton, also your extraordinary adventures and escape into the Union lines, came to hand only yesterday. I have been away from Charleston upon military duty for some time in the interior of Georgia, and received it only on my return to Savannah. All I can tell you in regard to your wife is, that I know, from friends in Columbia, she is alive, but shall write and make particular inquiries, and forward to you all details I can learn in regard to the young lady you have been so fortunate to win, as soon as they are sent to me.

Hoping you are having a more comfortable time in Nassau than you had on Morris Island, I am,

Yours, sincerely,

STUART BEE.

This letter kept me anxious but quiet in Nassau.

About the middle of September an additional note came from Bee which ran as follows :

SAVANNAH, GA., *Sept.* 4, 1864.

MY DEAR BRYANT : I have just received news from Columbia in answer to the inquiries I made with regard to your wife. She is alive, but I fear not having a very pleasant time with some of her relatives in regard to her marriage with you, and I think from what I hear, somewhat of an invalid, though from all I can learn her disease is not at all dangerous, and nothing that need to give you any immediate alarm. I write you the plain facts of the case as I get them. Would have been able to obtain them sooner, but everything at present seems to be disorganized in the Confederacy, postal service as well as other things. Don't let this make you anxious enough to attempt to visit her, for I assure you if you are caught again in this part of the world you will have very little chance of escaping this time.

Yours once more,

STUART BEE.

Whether Bee's warning would have had any effect upon me, I do not know. I was becoming desperate, and ready to take desperate chances ; in fact, had almost engaged my passage on a blockade-runner for the Confederacy, when, about the middle of October, I received a letter from my old chum Baxter, who held a staff position in Sherman's army, and with whom I had opened a correspondence. His letter was to the point, and read :

ATLANTA, GA., *Oct.* 8, 1864.

MY DEAR BRYANT : Your various letters to me seem to indicate that your anxiety in regard to your wife has become a mania with you. I have no doubt that the lady is well, and some of her friends may have intercepted the correspondence between you. If you wish to see her personally, the best way you can take is to join us. I am in a position to know now of a movement that will take this army very near to her. I am not at liberty to say more, and you will regard this as confidential. Come to Atlanta as soon as possible, and I will get you an appointment of some kind that will enable you to accompany the army ; but come at once, as very shortly the railroad behind us will be cut and communication will be severed between us and the outer world.

Your old friend,

THOMAS BAXTER.

After reading this letter carefully, I canceled my agreement for a passage on the blockade-runner, and two days afterward saw me on the steamer bound to New York. Making a few hurried preparations, I took the railroad for Nashville, and then pushed forward to Atlanta, where Hood and Sherman were at present confronting each other.

Here everything seemed to be in preparation for some great military movement. The divisions of Sherman's army were rapidly filling up; recruits being hastened to the front, and men and officers on furlough or leave of absence being called in. The train which carried me to Atlanta brought a large number of them.

After some trouble, I found the headquarters of the general's staff, and there met my friend Baxter. The mutual confidences incidental to the reunion of old chums being over, he laughed and said : " Got your carpet-bag with you, old boy ? "

" To go where ? " I asked.

" With us to the sea ! You want to find your wife. There is only one way of your getting to South Carolina, and that is with this army. We will soon cut loose from our base, and Heaven knows what will be our next one. Now," he continued, " if you want to go with us, you have got to become one of us."

" What ! " I said, " shoulder a musket ? "

" No, shoulder a staff appointment. Come with me."

He led me in to the chief of Sherman's staff.

That officer said, " Mr. Bryant, Major Baxter tells me you are an engineer, and should be very well acquainted with most of the Georgia railroads."

" Yes," I replied, " I have assisted in building a good many of them."

" Then," he remarked, " you should know how to destroy them,—their vital places, where the burning of a bridge will do the most damage, or the destruction of a culvert cause a wash-out of the track. We expect to destroy a great many railroads on this trip, and if you wish to accept an appointment on some division or brigade commander's staff, I will get it for you."

I replied that that would suit me very well, and two days afterward found me acting as extra aide-de-camp to Major-General Woods, commanding the first division of Logan's Fifteenth Army Corps, temporarily in charge of Osterhaus.

By November 12th, the last locomotive and train of cars had steamed out of Atlanta. These gone, we burned the railroads leading to the north, to prevent their being used by the Confederates. Thus cut off from all supplies, communication, and reinforcements, we had only the power of our sixty thousand veterans to rely on. But keep them in bread and meat, and they were the kind of men to go anywhere and do anything. On the 14th, with as little baggage, ammunition, and general army stores as it was considered possible for this great army to move with, we left Atlanta, marching southward, our next base of supplies we hoped to gain being Savannah, two hundred and odd miles away on the sea. I do not intend to give many details of that eventful march. I paid very little attention to the military movements about me, except so far as obeying my orders, and fulfilling my duties. But one thought dominated my mind, and that was that each mile that army traveled carried me a mile nearer to my wife.

Passing through the rich grain lands of central Georgia we lived as Caucus expressed it, "like fightin' chickens," my table being bounteously supplied by him ; for this creature was now in his element ; bringing a large youthful experience of water-melon raids and turkey-stalks to bear on the subject, as he expressed it, " of fightin' for de grub." The most expert " bummer " of Sherman's army looked with envy upon Caucus and his extraordinary contributions to our larder. Sometimes he would come in riding a " borrowed " horse, a turkey and goose slung over his shoulder, a sack of grain or potatoes on one side, a few strings of dried apples twisted around his neck, and driving a fat pig or plump calf ahead of him.

Passing through these rich plains of central Georgia, pontooning the rivers, the bridges having been destroyed, doing a little skirmishing, and in one or two places some hard fighting, and all the time destroying the railroads that were as vital to the existence of the Confederacy as arteries to the life of man, toward the end of November we arrived at the rice lands of Georgia. By this time the army consisted of three divisions. First, the regular army, disciplined and practiced, that kept their ranks, obeyed their orders, and did the fighting.

Next the bummers, stragglers, and worthless men of all corps, who were good—as Caucus expressed it—" only to do fightin' for de grub."

Then an immense concourse of negroes, who had left their homes and followed the army that had brought them freedom. These furnished a more serious impediment to us, almost, than the Confederates. They ate up everything they could put their teeth on, and as the army was compelled to depend for its existence upon the country through which it passed, if we had had another hundred miles to march through the rice swamps of Georgia, I doubt if many would have avoided starvation ; for the bummers got the best of all foraged provisions, the first pick of the barn-yards, and grain-cribs ; the enormous gangs of contrabands the rest ; and the army who did the fighting had a chance at what was left, which, as Caucus remarked, was " de last pick ob de bone ! "

However, in December we arrived in sight of the sea, and on the 13th, Fort McAllister having been captured by assault, we were in communication with the Federal fleet. A few days afterward we entered Savannah, which was evacuated by the Confederates under Hardee. But here disappointment and delay awaited me. Sherman, to complete his arrangements, reorganize his army, and obtain fresh supplies and ammunition, remained over a month in Savannah.

Every day I had marched, I had said, "So many miles nearer to Laura."

Fancy my impatience !

During this time, I made all the inquiries I could in Savannah in regard to the Peytons, but could learn nothing new. The old Confederate inhabitants had nearly all left the town, and those who remained had but little to tell me. However, I heard frequently of Mr. Amos Pierson. Unable to obtain the money due him from the Confederate Government in any other shape, he had received a large amount of cotton in payment of his claims, preferring that bulky but valuable merchandise to Confederate money that was now almost worthless. Most of this cotton had been shipped into South Carolina before the approach of Sherman's army, and stored at Columbia. I had no doubt that Mr. Pierson would be near his merchandise, and consequently near my wife. This made me more anxious than ever to be by her side.

But about January fifteenth Sherman made his preparations to leave Savannah for his campaign in South Carolina. The army had been "fighting light" when we left Atlanta, but now it might be called "flying light." Only the absolute necessities for the campaign were permitted us. The wounded, sick, and non-competent of every class were left behind.

On the seventeenth this movement really began, but it was delayed by tremendous rains that flooded the swamps in the vicinity of Savannah until January thirtieth, when the columns were fully in motion.

In Georgia we had destroyed railroads; during the march through South Carolina we built roads. Day after day I directed companies of men laying down corduroys over swamps and floating pontoons across rivers. Some idea of the herculean labor of the engineer corps of the army may be formed from the fact that we bridged the Salkehatchie River, which has fifteen different channels, between sunrise and sunset. Thus fighting battles and building bridges, we struggled through the swamps and morasses, and on the sixteenth day of February, 1865, looking across the Saluda River, saw the beautiful capital of South Carolina. While assisting in our preparations to bridge the river I could almost see Judge Peyton's home, and fondly imagined I saw the form of my beloved wife, whose face I had longed for but never seen for fourteen months.

Next morning in spite of considerable opposition from detachments of Confederate troops, the Fifteenth Corps succeeded in laying pontoons and crossing the river. Then skirmishing began. for the advance guard of Woods' Division, and was followed up by additional brigades being put in action, and the Confederates being driven over two miles. From their last position they retreated, and the mayor of Columbia with a number of the leading citizens came out to surrender the place to us. While negotiations for this were going on, Caucus, who probably knew the hen roosts of the neighborhood very well, had been out on a foraging expedition in the company of several more of the same kidney. About two o'clock he came riding in on horseback in a tremendous state of excitement, and coming to me cried : "Golly, Massa Bryant, if you want to save Judge Peyton's house you come along right smart."

"What do you mean?" said I.

"Dat swearin' colonel of Kilpatrick's Cavalry what brags dat he leaves only de chimneys and neber de houses, has gone up Judge Peyton's way, an' if you want to take care ob your wife's family you had better go quick."

The negro seemed very much excited and grieved to think of the fate that might come to his old master. I hardly noted this, however, for I rode at once to Division Headquarters. General Woods was seated on his horse.

I said: "General, can I have leave of absence for the day and also use a company of infantry?"

He looked at me inquiringly, as I had never made any such request before, and replied: "What for?"

"To protect my wife!"

At this the General nearly fell off his horse in astonishment, and gasped: "Your wife a South Carolinian, who lives here? You must be a South Carolina Unionist: By George! I should think you did deserve protection."

Explaining to him the peculiar relations I bore to Judge Peyton's family, he wrote an order directing a company of Stone's brigade to go with me.

As they filed off the captain remarked, for he had been placed under my orders for this expedition: "What do you want us for? Do you know of any treasure hid in the neighborhood?"

I explained to him my errand. He then said: "That's right, I've got a wife myself in Iowa. Boys, we'll follow him lively!" and gave his men the order to "double quick."

Guided by Caucus, we took a short cut. I had already had the protection signed by the division commander for Judge Peyton and his family.

Though we moved rapidly, we were not too soon.

Riding up the broad avenue of oaks, every tree of which reminded me of the beautiful girl I had left behind me, my heart bounding with exultation and hope, I galloped up to the house and found it in possession of the Federal soldiers.

Not heeding the marauders that were swarming over the rooms I remembered so well, I only thought of finding Laura or some one who could tell me of her.

The negro servants had all fled from the house but one that Caucus brought in from the garden, knew him and was not afraid of him. In answer to our questions she said Judge Peyton's family fearing what was now taking place, had gone into Columbia for protection that afternoon just before the cavalry rode up.

I asked if they were all well.

"Yes, Massa, all well."

This brought from me a sigh of relief and a " Thank God ! "

There was nothing now for me to do but to save the Judge's property, which I did with considerable trouble. Even after showing the protection signed by General Wood, one of the cavalry remarked : "Yes, that is to protect Judge Peyton's property, but these 'ere goods is now our property."

Had it not been for the captain of infantry, who swore the cavalry should obey orders, if he had to shoot every one of them, the troopers would have left very little of Judge Peyton's house.

All this took considerable time, and it was nearly five o'clock in the afternoon when I succeeded in making the proper arrangements. The captain of infantry left a sergeant and a squad to guard the house over night. Then I turned into the main road to Columbia.

Not wishing to travel entirely alone, as skirmishers and Confederate cavalry might be about, I was compelled to take the time that the tired infantry could march in, and it was becoming dusk when we reached Columbia.

The city we could see was already occupied by Federal troops; the flag of the Union flying from the State House.

The main street was now full of large quantities of cotton and other articles, dry goods, merchandise, etc., which had been taken out ready to be placed on trains to follow the Confederates ; this our rapid advance had prevented. The owner of the cotton I incidentally learned was my friend, Amos Pierson. This would doubtless be confiscated, and Mr. Pierson shorn of a great deal of his power and wealth. I was compelled to go to division headquarters to make my report. Here, to my astonishment, I heard that Amos Pierson, on the entry of our troops, had taken the oath of allegiance to the Federal Government, and claimed his cotton as a non-combatant.

Long before this I had dispatched Caucus to try and find out where Judge Peyton had taken his family.

My report being made, I was now free to seek my wife myself. In a fever of excitement I went to the houses at which I thought it likely she would be. Elbowing my way through streets full of excited boys in blue, who had unfortunately, either by design or accident, obtained a large amount of Confederate whisky, which had excited them still more, I sought my wife without success. Some of the people I called on had left the town ; the others had not seen the Peytons, and were too nervous about their own affairs to care much for those of any one else.

All this time with cheers and cries the soldiers paraded the streets in squads—even a strong provost-guard having but little control over them, the citizens looking at them, some with scowls and a few with joy on their faces from the surrounding houses and gardens. I went back to headquarters to wait impatiently for Caucus to report where I could find my wife, for without some definite knowledge I might have wandered for days—perhaps weeks—in that motley throng, and never have seen her ; for no ladies were walking the streets of Columbia that night.

While doing this I was surprised and astonished to hear a very violent commotion. Looking out of the window I saw a faint glow down the main street. This gradually became larger and larger, and the accompanying noise louder and more violent. Hurrying out, I, to my horror, saw a portion of the city was in conflagration. A very heavy wind added to its violence, while drunken soldiers, bummers and camp followers crazy with drink, spread the flames. A sudden fear darted through me. What, in a burning town full of drunken soldiers, in the dead of the night, would be the fate of my wife ? I must find her now !

The flames roared more fiercely than ever, the public buildings catching fire. Down the main street immense piles of cotton became each a huge bonfire, the wind carried the flaming flakes for blocks around, spreading the fire over a large portion of the city. Inaction was impossible to me. I was about to run blindly seeking her, when Caucus came panting to headquarters.

"Where is she?" I cried.

"Don't know sah! But tink Miss Laura's at Colonel Pickens. Nancy Jackson said dat dey was 'spected dar!"

I was already running in that direction, for the Pickens mansion was in almost the center of the burning district!

CHAPTER XX.

THE LITTLE HOSTAGE.

FOLLOWING Caucus through the streets of the city, wildly jostling drunken soldiers and citizens trying to save their household goods, we plunged into the burning portion of the town, and arrived at the Pickens mansion. This, being surrounded by a garden, I had hoped might have escaped, but it was also in flames. The family had fled from it, taking with them what possessions they could carry.

Inquiring of some negroes who were trying to save their household goods, they hurriedly told me that the Peytons had been there, but being driven out by the flames, had left about half an hour before. I asked which way. They pointed along another street, but gave little attention to me; they were too busy trying to save a little of their possessions from the wreck. Fighting my way through the throng with one idea—to find my wife and aid her—I was suddenly arrested by a crowd even more dense than that through which I had passed.

At this moment Caucus stopped and cried out, "Golly! Look at dat chile!"

"What do you mean?" said I. "Come along and help me find my wife."

As I uttered this, my attention was arrested by a shriek that apparently came from above me. Looking through the trees of a small garden, I perceived a house which was rapidly becoming a mass of flames.

At one of the upper windows of this a mulatto servant girl, holding in one arm a child, apparently white, was gesticulating wildly with the other and calling for assistance. My wife was probably safe, while this girl and her child were in mortal danger. For a moment I hesitated ; then dashed into the garden to save them.

I had had some experience in my youth as a member of a volunteer fire company, and calling to Caucus to follow me, I pushed through the crowd up to the house. No one was in the yard but negroes, and they were so panic-stricken that they had lost their wits, and though yelling and howling like madmen, were doing nothing to aid this woman in her extremity. With a ladder I could have rescued her easily, but there seemed to be none at hand. Bolting into the house, I tried the stairway, but it was burning and impossible to ascend. As I did so, the girl screamed and groaned, probably merely from terror, as the flames had not yet reached her, though this would be but a matter of a very few moments.

As I ran around the building trying to find a ladder by which to reach the upper windows, I caught sight of a tree at the other end of the house. The branches of this overhung the burning dwelling. Being a live oak, and green, this had not caught fire. If I could descend from its branches to the house I might save her. Looking around for a rope, my eye caught sight of the garden hose that had been used against the flames and then deserted. This I took, and Caucus, who was an expert climber, joining me, we both had little difficulty in reaching a branch of the tree immediately over the house.

Using the hose as a rope, I descended onto the roof of the veranda just in time, and breaking open one of the windows, sprang into the room, which was now full of suffocating smoke. Seizing the child from the almost fainting girl, I carried it to the roof and passed it up to Caucus as he reached down from the limb of the tree.

The rescue of the mulatto girl was more difficult. She seemed to have lost entirely the use of her limbs from ter-ror, but the roaring of the flames made me think quickly, and knotting the hose about her I climbed up it again to the tree. Then Caucus and I, using this hose as a rope, succeeded in swinging her off the veranda, and lowering her to the ground below. Unfortunately the hose, which was rotten, broke ; and the girl's descent, for the last few feet, was very rapid.

As we did this, a low moan or scream came from the street in front of the house, apparently from a woman.

The little baby, I could now see by the red glow of the fire, was white. The mulatto girl was probably its nurse. Holding the little infant tenderly in my arms, I descended the tree carefully but rapidly, as the flames were making my perch very warm and uncomfortable. As I did so, the child, which had been asleep, opened its arms and gave a little crow.

Caucus having gotten the girl on her feet, she recognized and spoke to him, and the negro ran frantically out to the street, before I had descended. A minute after he returned, his eyes rolling, his teeth jabbering with excitement, crying :

" Sah, dar's a lady in de street what would like to tank you for savin' her baby."

" Take the child to her," replied I, and was about to hand it to him. " Then come with me. My wife again demands every effort of mine."

" But, sah, de lady 'sists on seein' you."

With this he ran along, clapped his hands and crowed, then came back to me and chuckled, " Golly, don't em look like em daddy ! " and jabbered and poked the infant under the chin until I thought he had gone crazy.

But at this moment, an old gentleman, whose face by the light of the burning buildings made me start, came rapidly up to me, seized me by the hand and said, " Though you wear the uniform of the United States, let me thank you for what you have done for my family. My daughter here desires to thank you and bless you for saving her child."

" Yes, and I thank him, too," cried a girlish voice that seemed familiar, " though he is a Yankee."

I gave a stare. Miss Belle was standing near me. The other lady, the mother of the child, was murmuring blessings on my head, extending her hands to take her baby from me, but as she did so I gave a cry of startled joy.

Her eyes, bent down upon her infant to see that it was entirely safe, at this were lifted to mine. She gave a stifled shriek, " Lawrence ! " and fell fainting, but I caught her to my heart as there thrilled through me a wave of ineffable tenderness and supreme joy, for something sang in my brain that I had *my* wife and *my* child in my arms at the same moment.

As for the rest of them, they stared like crazy people. The Judge faltered, " Great heavens ! " while Miss Belle cried out, " Her husband ! " and seemed almost as much overcome as her sister, though she did not come to me and take my hand as she had been about to, when Laura recognized me.

The Judge, after a moment, said suddenly : " Law-rence, you came just in time. Get your wife and child away from here ; then I'll talk to you."

This we did, the Judge explaining to me the accident by which my little baby had been endangered. Driven away by the flames from the Pickens house, my wife, not having the strength to support the child herself, had taken a mulatto girl to carry it. This girl, in the struggling crowd, had got lost, though Laura ran about the streets like a mad woman trying to find her. Being frightened, the girl had taken refuge from some drunken soldiers, and gone up in the second story of the house, which was deserted by its owners, to be further away from the brutes, mad with whisky, who were following her. In her terror she had not discovered that the house was burning, until too late to escape by the stairs.

While the Judge was telling me this, Laura had partly regained her senses, and clung to me in that nervous, appealing manner which shows a man that a wife knows her husband is by her side.

We had now got out of the immediate vicinity of the fire, and I told the Judge of having saved his home from the marauding cavalry.

Obtaining a pass and escort from headquarters, and Caucus procuring an old wagon and pair of army mules, about twelve o'clock at night we all returned once more to the Oaks.

During this time Miss Belle had not said one word to me, although she looked at me very often, and some-times her glance seemed to me to be that of shame, which was very unusual in this young lady, as she was not accustomed to begging anybody's pardon under any circumstances. However, I was too busy to think of Belle. I had my child and my wife, who told me in a few hurried words that anxiety for my safety had made her sick. That her brother and father, after learning of her marriage, had always been kind to her, but that Miss Belle for six or seven months had never spoken to her, and had only become reconciled to her when her approaching motherhood had made her very feeble. "But then, Lawrence, Belle became an angel!" murmured Laura, "and nursed me like the kind sister she had always been before. She will forgive you, Lawrence, in time. You saved the baby, and Belle adores it, and that will make her tender to you some day."

The next morning I rode in to division headquarters, and after telling the general my story, he laughed and said : "After such a separation, you had better remain with your wife."

"That is impossible," I returned. "In a day or two the army leaves here, and I have got to go with it to the front."

"Not at all," he replied. "We must leave a garrison in this place, and I think I can get you detailed for that duty. You have been away from your wife for a long time, and you may as well remain as somebody who has no ties in Columbia. Besides, you are acquainted with the inhabitants here ; they knew you before the war, and General Sherman wishes to establish a good feeling between the troops in garrison and the people in the place. This fire has probably made them very bitter toward him, though we consider that it was not our doing, as the disaster began by the burning cotton, which was fired by the Confederate cavalry to prevent it from falling into our hands. As to the loss of the cotton, I am not at all sorry for it. It belonged to Amos Pierson, and the miserable turncoat took the oath of allegiance the first man in Columbia."

Two days afterward the bulk of Sherman's army marched out toward North Carolina, to make the closing campaign of the war. News came back from it day by day of its further advance and further success.

The loss of his cotton, however, made Mr. Amos Pierson a very poor man.

A few days afterward I had reason to know of this, because the old Judge called me into his study and asked my advice.

He said : "Mr. Bryant—or rather, Lawrence—you are

now one of my family ; the only male member of it that I can speak to on this matter. My son is away in the Confederate army in North Carolina, and as for the girls, they have no head for business. Two years ago I was compelled to mortgage this place, for the necessities of my family, to Mr. Amos Pierson for twenty-five thousand dollars. The note falls due to-morrow, and he demands payment of the same."

Twenty-five thousand dollars seemed to me a big sum for a moment, but when I reflected that it was in Confederate money, it almost dwindled to nothing when resolved into greenbacks.

I looked over the note, and found that it was a specific contract to pay twenty-five thousand dollars in the "lawful money of the Confederate States of America," and secured by a mortgage upon "The Oaks."

At this I gave a laugh, and said : "I will attend to this matter. It is not difficult to obtain twenty-five thousand dollars in Confederate money now. This fifty-dollar United States bill, I think, will cover your mortgage. The Confederate States are still a government *de facto*, and this is a specific contract. If you will come with me, we will make the tender in due form."

The next day accompanied by Caucus, who wheeled twenty-five thousand dollars in Confederate shinplasters alongside of us in a wheelbarrow, we went into Columbia, and going into Mr. Pierson's office, for the second time in my life, I saw the gentleman who had given me a great deal of trouble.

He was looking very miserable, for the war had dealt very hardly with him, and the loss of his cotton seemed to be almost the finishing blow. He smiled, however, upon our entrance, and was quite pleased to receive the money that Judge Peyton owed him. But on my tendering it to him in Confederate currency, he literally gave a shriek, and demanded bills of the United States of America as being the only legal tender then due.

Upon my explaining to him the specific nature of the contract, and making tender for same, and calling in several citizens and a notary public to witness this same tender, and sealing the Confederate shinplasters up in his presence, having counted them, he became abusive. "You ex-convict!" he cried, "didn't I put you on

Morris Island in a striped dress? I'll put you in a striped dress again,—a very different uniform from the fancy blue you now wear!—the accursed uniform that has ruined me!"

At this, Morris Island and all my wrongs at his hands rose up in me. I forgot myself, and after hammering Mr. Pierson in a way that made Caucus cheer with joy, I kicked him out of his own office, and never felt happier in my life than at the day's work I had done.

This tender of Confederate money of course brought on litigation that has not been ended to this day,—the Judge holding on to his homestead. Mr. Pierson still has twenty-five thousand dollars in Confederate money sealed up awaiting his order.

During these few weeks Miss Belle never spoke to me. Sometimes as I passed her she would give a little shudder and shrink away, not with horror or loathing, but rather it seemed to me with shame.

I had questioned my wife with regard to the numerous letters and draft I sent her. To my astonishment she said: " I never received a line from you, Lawrence, but have written you many, many times. This has had as much to do with my illness as anything else—my anxiety for you, and my fear that you might be dead, for I felt sure you would write me if you were alive."

I explained to her the various methods I had taken to communicate with her, and she seemed very much astounded.

" Surely," she cried, " some one of them must have reached me. Some letter from me should certainly have found you. And the draft ! What can have become of that ? "

I inquired at the bank in Columbia upon which I had received the exchange, and found that though they had advices of same, no such draft had yet been presented.

I held several conversations with my wife with regard to this, but we were never able to fathom it. I spoke to the Judge,—he knew nothing about it.

" I'll speak to Belle about it. She's had full charge of the household while I have been sick," said Laura.

But I remarked, " Better let the matter drop." Whether it was something in my manner gave my wife a suspicion I know not ; but she burst out at me : " You don't think my sister would do such a thing? You don't think my sister would be mean enough to withhold a husband's letters from his wife, or a wife's from her husband?"

"No," I said, "I don't. I don't care what has happened to the letters, Laura, since I have you and our child now, and that is enough for me!"

Whether Belle overheard this conversation or not I do not know, but I was sitting out in the grounds the next morning when that young lady came to me. Her face was very red, and her hands trembled.

I said, "Good-morning, Belle," as I always addressed her though she had never yet spoken to me.

Then she cried out: "How can you treat me so well, when I used to hate you so?"

"Used to?" I said.

"Yes," she replied. "But I have forgiven you since you saved the baby—my dear little nephew."

"Oh," I laughed, "Belle, I don't think you ever hated me very much."

"Didn't I?" she cried. "Look at these! These will tell you how I hated you, and how much I am ashamed of myself."

Then the girl burst out sobbing as she dropped a packet of letters into my hand. They were those from my wife to me and those I had written to her, all of them unopened.

"Now," she muttered, "I want to speak to you if you can ever forgive me. I want to ask one favor whether you forgive me or not. In my hate for you and my rage at my sister having married one of our enemies, I have done something that will make my sister despise me; perhaps also my father and brother. They are noble; they do not sneak about and steal letters as I did, and watch for them. Now I want to keep my sister's love. If you tell her, I am afraid I will lose it. You are a Northern man, and your side has conquered. You have every-thing—have pity also. Leave me my sister's love." And she commenced to sob more bitterly than ever.

"Miss Belle," I said, "why don't you ask for a brother's love?"

"Your love?" she gasped.

"Yes," I said, and put my hand upon hers, but as I did so she caught sight of my blue uniform, and cried,

"Not yet!" Then after a pause the girl continued:
"You have been very noble to me, and perhaps it will
come in time. If the North is as noble and magnanimous
as you are to me, perhaps the North and South may yet
be brother and sister," and ran away from me.

But every day after this she became more friendly, and
when her brother came home after Johnston's surrender,
even his empty sleeve did not make her take her hand
off my shoulder as we all, from the piazza, watched him
ride up the avenue of oaks to be clasped in his father's
arms.

Soon after this my gallant friend Bee, who had done so
much to bring Laura and me together, on his way to
Georgia from Lee's surrendered army stopped to spend
a few days with us. He was going back to a ruined
plantation, a deserted home and a wrecked fortune, but
he was the same gallant *débonnaire* Georgian as ever,
and he laughed and said, as he bade us good-by : "Perhaps when I get a home and something to eat in Georgia,
I may come back to see you again. I presume by that
time I will need a wife."

Here he looked at Miss Belle, who blushed very deeply
and went silently into the house.

So we began our life over again. There were plenty
of railroads to rebuild in the South, and the value of my
farm in Illinois made me quite rich at that time and in
that region of country.

And while doing so the stragglers from the Confederate
army gradually dropped into their old places one by
one—those that were left of them. Then one day my
wife said to me as we sat on the old porch of "The
Oaks," the Judge smoking a Havana cigar now, instead
of his old corncob, and Caucus at the other end of the
veranda chuckling to our little boy, who was crowing at
him in the arms of Miss Belle, "Most of our soldiers
are home now, but Major Harry Walton has never returned, and I have not heard of him for nearly a year.
Can he be one of the dead ? "

On this, I told my wife the story of her letter ; how
it had saved my life ; how Walton had loved her too
much to make her a widow, and had died fighting for the
cause he loved and believed in, as so many more Southern
gentlemen did in those four years of war. And as my

words disclosed to Laura the unselfish love of the dead Confederate for her, and what it had done for me, she clung to me and murmured :

"Lawrence, we have not christened our boy yet. Let us call him by the name of the man who gave his father life while he found death. Let us call him Harry Walton Bryant."

FINIS.

OPINIONS OF

THE GREAT NOVEL,

Mr. Barnes

of New York.

ENGLAND.

"There is no reason for surprise at 'Mr. Barnes' being a *big hit*."—*The Referee*, London, March 25th.

"*Exciting and interesting.*"—*The Graphic.*

"'Marina Paoli'—a giant character—just as strong as 'Fedora.'"—*Illustrated London News.*

"A capital story—most people have read it—I recommend it to all the others."
—JAMES PAYNE in *Illustrated London News.*

AMERICA.

"Told with the genius of Alexander Dumas, the Elder."—*Amusement Gazette.*

"Have you read 'MR. BARNES OF NEW YORK?' If no, go and read it at once, and thank me for suggesting it. . . . I want to be put on record as saying 'it is the best story of the day—the best I have read in ten years.'"—JOE HOWARD in *Boston Globe.*

But at that time Mr. Howard had not read

"Mr. Potter of Texas."

THE MOST EXTRAORDINARY,
THE MOST EXCITING,
THE MOST MARVELOUS
STORY EVER WRITTEN,

A Florida

Enchantment.

By
ARCHIBALD CLAVERING GUNTER,

Author of

"MR. BARNES OF NEW YORK,"

"MR. POTTER OF TEXAS,"

"THAT FRENCHMAN!"

"MISS NOBODY OF NOWHERE," etc.,

and

FERGUS REDMOND.

FOR SALE EVERYWHERE.

THE HOME PUBLISHING CO.,

NEW YORK.

Mr. Potter
of Texas.

AMERICAN EDITION,

170,000.

ENGLISH EDITION,

100,000.

"The description of the Bombardment of Alexandria, in 'Mr. Potter of Texas,' is, perhaps, the most *stirring picture* painted by the pen of any writer *in several generations.*"

OPINIONS OF

THE GREAT NOVEL,

Mr. Barnes

of New York.

ENGLAND.

"There is no reason for surprise at 'Mr. Barnes' being a *big hit.*"—*The Referee*, London, March 25th.

"*Exciting and interesting.*"—*The Graphic.*

"'Marina Paoli'—a giant character—just as strong as 'Fedora.'"—*Illustrated London News.*

"A capital story—most people have read it—I recommend it to all the others."
—JAMES PAYNE in *Illustrated London News.*

AMERICA.

"Told with the genius of Alexander Dumas, the Elder."—*Amusement Gazette.*

"Have you read 'MR. BARNES OF NEW YORK?' If no, go and read it at once, and thank me for suggesting it . . . I want to be put on record as saying 'it is the best story of the day—the best I have read in ten years.'"—JOE HOWARD in *Boston Globe.*

But at that time Mr. Howard had not read

"Mr. Potter of Texas."